ACKNOWLEDGMENTS

Thank you especially to all of my readers for supporting this series! I couldn't do it without you. And a special thanks to all of my editors–Julie, Kay, and Christine.

My fellow hockey players. Thanks for always giving me material and awesome, pun-tastic one-liners.

And my family. Thanks for always supporting me and my books! I'm so lucky to be able to do what I love and for you guys to have my back.

Love you guys!
—XOXO,
E

BENCHED

GOLD HOCKEY BOOK 4

ELISE FABER

BENCHED
BY ELISE FABER

BENCHED
Copyright © 2019 Elise Faber
Print ISBN-13: 978-1946140-25-8
Ebook ISBN-13: 978-1-946140-24-1
Cover Art by Jena Brignola

For Noah.
Because you're as special as they come.

GOLD HOCKEY SERIES

Blocked

Backhand

Boarding

Benched

Breakaway

Breakout

Checked

PROLOGUE

Max

MAX STOOD on the perimeter of the crowd, edging toward the door.

Yes, he was an asshole to escape in this moment, but Blane and Mandy wouldn't miss him.

Plus, he'd been here for the big event, after all.

No one would even know he'd gone.

He cracked the door, slipped out into the hall . . . then nearly mowed down a tiny little fairy.

Okay, not so much a fairy as a woman with pale amber hair and a curvy little body. Some players were all about the statuesque model type, but not Max. *He* liked them curvy, and he certainly didn't mind them small.

That meant he could more easily lift them up, that they could wrap their legs around his hips while he—

Fuck. It had been a long time since he'd been with a woman.

And this tiny, voluptuous angel was trying to make a quick getaway.

"Hey," he said, snagging her arm when she would have slunk down the hall. "You lost, sweetheart?"

Shoulders straightened and she ripped out of his grip. "Don't touch me," she snapped, keeping her back to him, and *fuck*, even her voice made his cock twitch.

"Okay. No problem." He slid around to her front. "But this area is off limits."

Her gaze stayed on the floor, her jaw clenched tight. "I was invited."

"Oh?" Max crossed his arms, leaned back against the wall. Sexy voice, banging body—he was desperate now to see her eyes, the shape of her nose, her lips. Please, let her be as pretty as she sounded. "By who?"

Finally, she looked up.

Max sucked in a breath as though he'd been gut-punched.

Those eyes. They were—

"Mandy Shallows," the woman said. "I'm . . ." She hesitated then lifted her chin and said, "I'm her sister."

Mandy has a sister? Holy shit.

But something was off. Max took a step closer to her, noted that the tip of her nose was slightly rosy, her lids reddened and puffy. "Why don't I think those are happy tears for her engagement?"

The woman pushed around him, striding down the hall before stopping and hanging her head again. "I didn't mean to intrude," she said. "I—" Her voice caught. "She said anytime, but I should have called first. This wasn't mine to witness." A sigh. "If she saw, if she's upset, tell her I'm sorry."

She started walking again, this time faster.

"Wait," he said and caught her arm again. "I'm sure Mandy will be happy—"

"*No.*" She yanked out of his grip, her purse slipping down

her arm and falling to the floor. The contents went every which way.

"Shit," he muttered. "I'm sorry." He knelt to help her, but she batted his hands away.

"Just go, dammit! Just leave me the fuck alone."

"Okay—" he began but didn't get the chance to leave.

Because she'd snatched up her things and was gone.

Sighing, he turned back toward the PT Suite. He should probably face the music. Congratulate the couple, break the news of Mandy's sister running off.

He took a step and the crinkle made him freeze.

Max bent, picked up the paper that must have fallen out of the woman's purse. It was an email addressed to . . . Angelica Shallows.

ONE

Max

"DAAAAAAD!" Brayden yelled, crashing through the door to his bedroom. "It's time for school!"

Max opened his bleary eyes, wincing when the doorknob slammed into the wall. He'd already repaired a handle-shaped hole from that particular spot more than once. His son never moved in anything less than a sprint.

"Fuck," he muttered, stretching his arms above his head and blinking against the sunlight streaming into his bedroom.

"Fuck is a bad word," Brayden said, plunking onto the mattress and cuddling close to Max.

And that right there.

His baby boy burrowing into his side, bedhead on full display, bright blue eyes staring up at him made every single thing over the last seven years worth it.

"You're right, bud," he said. "Now, what's this about school?" Max reached an arm for his nightstand. "My alarm hasn't even gone off—"

Well, fuck.

It *was* time for school.

Okay, *past* time for school. As in, they were already late. But he'd set his alarm. Last night after stumbling into the house at a quarter past three—professional hockey players and flight delays upon returning from a five-game road trip did not make for a happy team—he remembered opening the clock app on his phone and setting the alarm for seven . . .

He glanced down at his phone screen.

"Fuck," he muttered again.

Because seven *P.M.* was *not* going to get them to school on time.

Brayden opened his mouth. "That's—"

"I know," Max said. "Bad word. Bad Dad." He clapped his hands together. "Okay, bud, so we've gotta move. You get your teeth brushed and shoes on. I'll meet you in the kitchen with a yogurt and cereal in three minutes, yeah?"

Brayden nodded, a soldier ready for battle, then took off down the hall.

Flinching at the sound of another door crashing into another wall—Brayden's bedroom this time—Max rolled out of bed, yanked on a pair of sweatpants, a sweatshirt, and a hat. He took thirty precious seconds to brush his teeth before shoving his feet into a pair of shoes, pounding down the stairs, and hustling through the hall to the kitchen.

Another slam indicated Brayden had moved on to brushing his teeth.

Max opened the fridge then scrambled to grab Brayden's Minecraft lunchbox—he needed to give his nanny a raise for having made it the night before—and snagged a yogurt pouch. Two seconds to snip the top of the yogurt tube, ten more to grab a cup and fill it with Cheerios, then a few more frustrating ones as he fought with the zipper on his son's overpriced *Jurassic Park* backpack before managing to stow his lunch inside.

He was breathing harder than after a shift on the ice by the time Brayden came in, shoes on, hair miraculously tamed, and smile wide.

"Anna"—their nanny—"taught me how to do my hair."

Max's heart clenched. With guilt for not being the one to teach his son, with anger that his ex hadn't been there to show Brayden either, with fury that she'd bailed and left them both with a giant hole that he had no clue how to fill.

Stuck in his head, in the memories of his ex-wife, Max had taken too long to reply to Brayden's statement.

His wide smile started to fade, the brightness in his eyes dimming.

Max hurried across the kitchen and scooped Brayden up. "It looks awesome, dude. Can you do mine like that when you get home from school?"

Brayden grinned and threw his arms around Max's neck. "Yup."

"Good." Max set him down. "You breakfast. Me backpack. Us car."

A giggle, but Brayden grabbed the makeshift breakfast and pushed through the door leading out to the garage. Max snagged the ridiculously expensive backpack—fine, he was still salty about spending over fifty bucks on a cheap-looking plastic covered bag with a zipper that rarely worked—but Brayden had loved it and his son rarely asked for anything.

Which meant that any time he *did* ask, Max caved like a chocoholic at a Hershey's convention.

Luckily, he only lived about ten minutes from Brayden's school, in a little suburb south of San Francisco, where his team, the Gold, was headquartered. They practiced and played in the city, but Max had wanted something a little quieter for his son, especially after the huge media storm that had resulted from his and Suzanne's separation.

He thanked social media for that one.

Namely, his wife's—*ex*-wife's—uncanny ability to relay every personal, painful, juicy, and often exaggerated detail of their lives . . . as well as including plenty of flat-out falsehoods on the Twitter-verse.

Fuck, if there were a person in the world he could hate, it was Suzanne.

But he couldn't, because she'd given him Brayden.

The rest of it, though, the lies, the scheming, the always-cry-wolf, *those* he could never forgive.

He started up the car, listening and chiming in at the right places as Brayden talked all things video game.

But his mind was unfortunately stuck on Suzanne and the fact that women were not to be trusted.

He snorted. Brit—the Gold's goalie and the first female in the NHL—and Mandy—the team's head trainer—would smack him around for that sentiment, so he silently amended it to: *most* women were not to be trusted.

There. Better, see?

Somehow, he didn't think they'd see.

He parked in the school's lot, walked Brayden in, and received the appropriate amount of scorn from the secretary for being thirty minutes late to school, then bent to hug Brayden.

"I'll pick you up today," he said.

Brayden smiled and hugged him tightly. Then he whispered something in his ear that hit Max harder than a two-by-four to the temple.

"If you got me a new mom, we wouldn't be late for school."

"Wh-what?" Max stammered.

"Please, Dad? Can you?"

And with that mind fuck of an ask, Brayden gave him one more squeeze and pushed through the door to the playground, calling, "Love you!" over his shoulder.

Then he was gone, and Max was standing in the office of his son's school struggling to comprehend if he had actually just heard what he'd heard.

A new mom?

Fuck his life.

TWO

Angelica

ANGIE SHUT down her computer and stood up from her desk with a groan. It was late, way later than she would normally work, but she'd been so close to figuring out the issue in her code that she'd been unable to quit for the day.

Not until she'd found the line that was causing the whole program to crash.

She rubbed bleary eyes as she waited for everything to shut down then picked up her cell and sent her boss, Sebastian, a quick text, letting him know all was now good with her part of the project.

Sebastian was technically on the Steele side of the RoboTech-Steele Technologies venture—as the former assistant of Clay Steele, the CEO himself—while Angie was on the RoboTech side—headed by Clay's wife, Heather O'Keith—so Sebastion wasn't quite her boss. But when the two CEOs had gotten married last year, their respective companies had begun several joint projects, and Sebastian was now in charge of making sure all of those endeavors, including the one she'd just finished, were running smoothly.

Angie normally wouldn't be this hands-on with a specific project, as she'd moved more into management over the last several years, but she'd recently brought on a new hire, in the form of a brilliantly talented woman named Kelsey.

Kelsey Scott was a few years older than her, but she was looking to move from the government sector back into the private one. RoboTech was funding one of her innovative proposals, which meant most of Angie's software engineers were otherwise occupied and couldn't take on the small project she'd just spent the last week tackling.

Well, sometimes being the boss meant she had to get her hands dirty.

And considering how long it had taken her to diagnose the simple problem with her code that day, it was clear she needed to get those mitts dusty a little more often.

Sebastian replied with a thanks followed by a message telling her it was too damn late and to go home.

On it, she sent back with a smiley face.

Sebastian was good people, and she'd enjoyed working with him over the last few months. He was fun, nice, and a ruthless taskmaster when needed.

Which was, more often than not, most of the time. Especially since the majority of his job included wrangling a multitude of different departments, numerous vendors, and, she had to face facts, stroking egos. Still, Sebastian was good at balancing all of that, and Angie had made it a point to file away some of his techniques for dealing with the *egos* in her own department.

Over the last few years, she'd largely done away with any troublemakers, but occasionally one of the older men liked to mansplain her job to her.

Annoying.

But unsurprising considering she was nearing thirty and still looked like she was eighteen.

For God's sake, her dad had been a six-foot-four, two-hundred-and-thirty-pound hockey player and she was what? A buck ten on a good day? Five-two rounding up?

She was short with a big ol' apple bottom and barely-there boobs. Her sister, on the other hand, was petite, but in all the right ways, perfectly hourglass with porcelain skin and gorgeous high cheekbones.

Angie had a hell of a time just finding jeans that fit.

Because life was . . . well, shit, it was really *lifey* sometimes.

Why had she thought about her sister? It had been close to four months since Angie had accidentally walked in on her engagement in progress, had almost ruined one of the few happy moments Mandy'd had in her turbulent and tragic life.

"Ugh," she muttered, grabbing her hoodie and shrugging into it. Her backpack followed suit and though she moved quickly toward the stairs, the thoughts of Mandy didn't fade so easily.

Thoughts about the email sent the previous year gently disclosing their shared father.

Followed up by an earnest plea to get to know one another.

Except, Angie already knew all about Mandy. She'd known her from her earliest moments, resented her sister for years, hated her, despised her until she'd known the truth.

See?

No.

And she hadn't either.

Because Angie hadn't been old enough to understand cheating and affairs and other families.

She'd only known what her mother had told her.

That Mandy and her mother had stolen her father away.

That the bare glimpses, the extremely brief visits he'd been able to make were their fault.

If *they* weren't there, Angie and her mother would have all the attention.

Thankfully, her phone buzzed at that moment, pulling her out of the rabbit hole of her brain and depositing her right back into the present.

Probably a robocall, since she'd done a damn good job of pushing away any friends she'd had over the last few years. Kind of hard to be a friend to someone when her entire childhood had morphed and twisted before her eyes.

God. Part of her wished she'd never found the NDA in her mother's paperwork.

It was ill to think of the dead, and that particular piece of paper had made it all but impossible *not* to.

"Hello," she said carefully, after swiping across the screen and putting her cell up to her ear. She started descending the stairs and was surprised to find a familiar voice on the other end of the call.

"It's Kelsey," said the woman. "I meant to catch up with you today then got distracted. I figured since it popped into my head now, I'd better take the chance to call." She laughed. "Sorry. Rambling. Anyway, a few of the other girls and I were going to meet up for a drink tomorrow. Do you want to come with?"

"Me?" she asked, reaching the ground floor and pushing through the door to the lobby.

"This *is* Angie, right?"

"Yeah."

She could almost hear the frown forming on Kelsey's face. "Then, yes, I want you to come."

"Oh."

"Is that—" A pause. "I mean, are drinks bad?" Kelsey's voice dropped. "I mean are you *not* drinking?"

Angie's lipped twitched. She'd gotten to know the other woman a little bit over the last months. Kelsey was nice, and it was her own brain and past that was pushing this conversation onto the wrong side of awkward.

"No," she said. "I am. Drinking that is."

Silence. Then, "Oh. Okay."

And Angie barely held back her groan.

"I'm sorry. I'm in a weird headspace," she admitted. "I'd love to grab a drink."

Look now, that wasn't hard, was it? Just accept the offer graciously and move on. Unfortunately for Angie, the rebuke came in the form of her mother's voice, and that just made everything so much worse.

She needed to end this call then go home and self-medicate with a carton of double fudge brownie ice cream.

Thankfully, Kelsey seemed to sense her discomfort, which couldn't be hard, especially considering how freaking weird Angie was being. Regardless, after the barest hesitation, Kelsey hung up with a cheerful, "See you tomorrow!"

"See you," Angie said. "Sorry, I'm so—"

The call had already ended.

G.R.O.A.N.

God. Why was she so weird?

Childhood trauma. Yup, there was that.

Or maybe because she was an engineer.

Yeah. Probably that, too.

THREE

Max

MAX STARED through the kennel door at the shelter and couldn't help but wonder what in the ever-loving fuck he was doing. Seriously. Was he really considering adopting a dog because he didn't want to have a tough conversation with his son?

Was he *that* crappy of a father?

"If you adopt that one," Anna said, "I will cut you with your own skate."

Yes. He'd called in the big guns. But Brayden asking for a new mom had definitely warranted the big guns. It was DEFCON 1 as far as he was concerned. And luckily, he and Anna had been discussing getting a dog for a while now, so this morning's visit to the shelter hadn't been totally unplanned.

Just accelerated by a seven-year-old's request and his own panic in dealing with the situation. Pussy? Yes. But also a new mom?

Fuck. No.

"You'd have to fight Richie"—the Gold's equipment

manager—"for my skates," he retorted. "He practically guards them under lock and key."

Anna crossed her arms. She was all of five feet nothing, but with long blond hair and piercing blue eyes that never failed to make him or Brayden behave. "I'd win."

Max grinned despite himself. "Yes. Yes, you would."

When she smiled and dropped her arms, he pointed back at the black and white pup inside the cage. "So, what's wrong with that one?" he asked.

"Um, hello Mr. Observant," she teased. "Aren't you supposed to be one of those really good players who reads the plays in the game before they develop?" She tapped one blue-painted fingernail to her chin. "Weren't you Playmaker of the Month, or something?"

"Player of the Month," he grumbled, still trying to figure out why the cute little pooch had raised his nanny's red flags.

"Still don't see it?" she asked and when he shook his head, she pointed to the back of the cage. "Pooped and peed inside, so not potty-trained yet. That's not disqualifying on its own, but he's also shredded his bed, so he has destructive tendencies that need to be addressed. Not to mention the manic look in his eyes and the amount of barking when we walked in." She ticked off on her fingers. "Destructive. Loud. High energy. Not housebroken. All things that you can train, but not with an owner who's out of town for a good chunk of the year and a nanny whose main responsibility is the child, not a dog."

Damn.

She was good.

"You're right," he muttered. "Annoying as shit but still right."

Anna clasped her hands to her chest, fluttering her eyelashes. "You're so good to me."

He narrowed his eyes. "You're not getting a raise."

A sigh, but her lips were twitching. "Damn. And I was trying so hard for one, too."

"Sure, you were," he said, moving on to the next kennel. This one held some sort of tiny white fluffy dog. Yeah, no. Not happening. He could practically hear the ribbing from the guys already. Next. "You and that smart mouth of yours. So, which one would you choose?"

Anna flicked her long blond ponytail over one shoulder and pointed to the end of the hall. "First, my smart mouth is why you hired me. I wasn't bending over backward to prostrate myself at the feet of the Hockey God. And second, if you *are* actually getting a dog today, I would go with that one." He trailed her to the kennel she'd indicated. "He's older, so less likely to be adopted. But he's also calm, housetrained, and his card says good with both kids and other animals."

Max tilted his head from side to side. "He's not much to look at."

The dog was medium-sized with dull brown fur that was patchy in places. Its eyes were set closely together, his tail misshapen, and one ear stood up while the other flopped to the side.

Anna punched his shoulder. "Neither are you."

His mouth twitched as he glanced at the card hanging on the outside of the door. The pup's name was apparently Sparky, not the greatest, but that could be changed. More importantly, the tag also proclaimed that Sparky was good with kids, other dogs, and even cats. His cage was clean, and his demeanor calm, almost bordering on reserved as Anna and Max watched him.

But more than that . . .

"Damn," he said, as he studied Sparky's face. Because the pup's eyes held a trace of sadness, as if he knew it was unlikely he would ever leave the shelter, that *this* was his future, to sit inside a sad and lonely cage for the rest of his meaningless and short life.

Fuck him, but that was maudlin.

"Damn what?" Anna asked.

He sighed. "I guess we're getting a dog today."

Anna smiled as she glanced down at her phone. "Well, you'd better get moving with the adoption if you're going to pick up Max on time. I'll step out to call the vet and get Sparky an appointment, so you can make sure all is good with him. Then we'll stop by the pet store and get him the essentials." She nodded, almost to herself, then pulled up her notes on her cell and started making a list of the essentials as she walked back down the hall.

"I have a vet?" he asked.

"I did some research when you told me this was a possibility."

"Damn," he muttered again.

Because that right there was why Anna was getting another raise.

FOUR

Angelica

WHY WAS SHE DOING THIS?

Or more importantly, *how* could she be doing this?

She had heels on, for God's sake. Heels and a dress and—

Angie pulled open the door to Bobby's Place and peeked in. Music blared from speakers, all pop-tastic and modern. Women with perfectly coiffed hair gathered in clusters around men who wore . . . really tight jeans and man buns and—

Nope. She *couldn't* do this. Fear coiled in her stomach, crept up her throat.

Yes, she was in a dress, but it was a dress with *Star Wars* characters on it. Yes, she had heels on, but they were adorned with buttons of her favorite droid. And all of that was covered, or nearly covered in the case of her heels, by her favorite, coziest, and somewhat frumpy sweater/cloak.

Yes, she said a sweater/cloak.

No, it wasn't just a sweater and it wasn't quite a cloak. It was a sweater/cloak—long and baggy like a cloak, but made out of a cozy knit that was as soft as cashmere.

Had she mentioned that she didn't have friends?

Angie risked one more peek inside, but nope, the trendy, gorgeous patrons hadn't transformed in the last thirty seconds into less attractive, more normal albeit nerdy humans.

They were still beautiful and outgoing and confident, and she was still . . . her.

She let the door go.

Turned to leave, but just as she did, the door popped back open and Kelsey's head appeared, whack-a-mole style.

"You're not leaving, are you?" she exclaimed.

Well, shit.

Angie scrambled, shaking her head. "Oh. *No*. Of course not. I . . . uh . . . just left my phone in my car and was going back to get it." She pointed a hand behind her, then realized it held her cell. She was. So. Smooth. Ugh. "Oh, never mind. Look at that. I've got it right here."

Kelsey studied her for a moment then smiled. "It's been a long week."

Angie smiled weakly, thankful for the bone being thrown her way. "*Really* long."

"Come on then," Kelsey said and took her arm. "You need a drink, but brace yourself, because we've got to wind our way through the models in the front room to where us normal folks hang out in the back."

"Normal—?" Angie started to ask, because Kelsey was absolutely gorgeous in her own right, but Kelsey had already opened the door and the rest of her sentence was drowned out by pulsing dance music.

Probably a good thing, considering her track record with making things awkward.

Some people got eidetic memory as their superpower.

Others could do math in a fraction of a second.

Angie?

Her superpower was making things weird.

Put that on a T-shirt and sell it.

Kelsey tugged her at a quick pace through the bar and down a hallway that had been invisible from the front door. Funny, that, not being able to see the whole picture of a place from a single glance—or two, rather.

Sigh. She really needed to get out more.

Anyway, Kelsey led her down the hall and through an open doorway that led into another bar.

Now *this* one was what Angie had pictured.

Warm wood coated the walls, several booths lined the perimeter of the room, stools covered in cheery red leather perched like drunken soldiers in front of the bar. All the wood was slightly worn, just on the right side of lived in.

Instantly, Angie's discomfort faded.

This was a place she could be comfortable in.

"Come on," Kelsey said with another tug. She pulled Angie toward a booth filled with women in the corner of the room. "Hi, girls," she announced. "This is Angelica Shallows."

"Angie," she said, extending her hand to shake each of the women's hands in turn. "It's nice to meet you all."

"Hi," a petite redhead with whiskey-colored eyes said. "I'm Kate."

"Heidi," said a brunette with striking hazel eyes.

A nod from the last. "Cora." Her smile was slightly wicked, and it matched her dark brown hair and eyes.

And . . . cue awkward.

"Thanks for letting me crash your get together tonight," Angie said, shifting from foot to foot as the silence extended.

Kelsey seemed to shake herself. "Scoot," she told Cora and all but shoved Angie into the booth. She grabbed a chair from a nearby table then plunked down into it. "Okay," she said. "Here's the rundown. I know Angie from work. Cora from elementary school. Kate and Heidi, we met in college."

"Met?" Heidi said with a smile. "You all but dragged me into your little circle."

Kelsey pointed a finger at her. "Worth it," she said. "We're awesome-sauce."

Cora wrinkled her nose. "Except when you use that word."

"Awesome-sauce?" Kelsey's brows drew together. "But that's a great word. It shows that I'm hip and—"

Kate interrupted. "We are definitely not hip. And we're all too old to use awesome-sauce in normal conversation."

"Come on," Angie said. "I mean, look at you guys, you're all beautiful and your clothes are amazing, and I'm all nerdy and dorky and weird."

Holy. Fucking. Shit.

She clamped both hands over her mouth because. She. Had. Not. Just. Said. That. Her cheeks flared red-hot, her throat tightened, and her eyes burned.

It was like she'd forgotten how to interact with other human beings.

What in the hell was wrong with her?

Ever since her sister had emailed her, ever since she'd seen Mandy's engagement, learned the truth of her sister's upbringing, Angie had been a wreck.

She started to stand. "I'm sor—"

"And damn, all that without a drink," Cora said, staying her motion with a hand on her arm. "Girl. We're *all* weird. Hell, I have an unhealthy affinity for unicorns, Kate is obsessed with Hermione Granger, Kelsey is freakishly smart, and Heidi, well don't get me started about Heidi. She's the absolute craziest of us all."

Heidi gasped then reached across the table to smack Cora across the shoulder. "What the hell?"

"You *are* weird." Cora shrugged. "It's just one of those things." She turned to Angie. "So, you. *Star Wars*, obvs. What else makes your freak flag fly?"

"Umm." Her voice was small. "Harry Potter? Reading? Cozy socks?"

"No." Cora tapped her chin. "You like those, but what really gets you hot?"

"Stop," Kelsey said. "She's new, give her a break."

Angie felt her lips curve, despite herself. "No, you're right. While I do love all those things, what I love more than all other things is *Star Wars*. I swear, I must have watched the original trilogy of movies several hundred times in high school. I'd come home from school and put on *Empire* or *Return of the Jedi* and I'd just . . . I don't know . . . believe that good could prevail over bad for a change."

Even if it was purely just fiction.

Because, God knew, good couldn't prevail in her own life.

She winced.

Heidi reached across the table and squeezed her hand. "I know just what you mean, and while I'm not a huge *Star Wars* fan, I can appreciate what it did for you. That's why we all love these fictional stories." A shrug. "For escapism. To hope for the fantasy and to forget how miserable our own lives are."

Yes. That exactly.

Angie smiled at her. "Thanks. It's nice to meet people who actually get it."

"We get you," Kelsey murmured. "We've all been there."

Cora laughed and lifted her beer. "Hence drinks."

Kate grinned, raising her own glass. "Or juice. We're all pretty easy here. You do you."

"I'll just go grab a rum and coke," Angie said, starting to stand again.

"Sit." Kelsey pointed at the bar. "I'll get this one—"

"I couldn't—"

"You can get the next round." And staying any further arguments, she pushed to her feet and hurried to the bar.

"And it'll only be one more round," Cora stage-whispered, "because we're all lightweights, so don't let her con you into a third."

"I'm in good company then," Angie replied. "Because any more than that, and I'll be hating myself in the morning."

"Not me," Kate teased, sipping from her glass of what appeared to be apple juice. "I can do more rounds than any of you guys combined."

"Juice." Cora tipped up the bottom of the cup, causing Kate to gulp and then nearly spit out her mouthful. "And you can't even drink that properly, so get out of here with that nonsense."

Kate wiped her chin before taking another drink, though a more dignified one this time, as it was complete with a raised pinky.

Heidi rolled her eyes.

"So, what are you into, Heidi?" Angie asked into the silence that descended. "I heard about freakish smarts and Hermione and unicorns. What's your secret—or not so secret—nerd-dom?"

Heidi took a sip of her cocktail. "*Twilight.*"

"She has a fantasy about vampires sucking her lady bits while she's on her—"

"Cora!"

"Barf," Kate said.

"Stop trying to shock Angie," Kelsey said, returning to the table and setting a glass down in front of her. "We're a lot to take in one sitting."

"*I'm* a lot—" Cora began.

"Yes," they all—including Angie—practically shouted.

Cora huffed, but she was grinning. Then Kate began sharing a funny story of Kelsey in college—young, super smart, with lots of naïveté thrown in. It made for plenty of hilarity and pretty soon they were in hysterics.

They stuck to the aforementioned two rounds—Angie buying the second round. Eventually, the bartender brought over a pitcher of water, and they laughed and teased each other and giggled like loons in that booth in the corner.

It was, hands down, the best night of Angie's life.

FIVE

Max

MAX SLIPPED on his helmet and stood. Brit, their starting goalie and the first female hockey player in the NHL, was standing by the door leading out of the locker room, mask on, stick in hand, and ready to lead them out onto the ice.

His nerves jangled like an overloaded set of car keys and his heart raced.

But it was always like this.

The game itself—the speed, the hits, the pucks, and the cold slap of the ice upon entering the arena. Max could not imagine doing anything else.

He fell into line behind Blane, slapping the forward on his shoulder.

Blue, the rookie who they really shouldn't be calling a rookie since he was on his third season in the big leagues but who they still labeled a rookie anyway because hockey and ribbing went hand in hand, tapped Max on the ass.

"Gonna give me some decent passes, old man?"

Max's lips twitched. "You gonna get open? Move those

teenaged legs for a change?"

"Fuck you."

"Fuck *you*."

Ah. Hockey.

He and Blue shared a grin before Max rotated back around and sucked in a breath.

Game time, motherfuckers.

Channeling his little slice of Samuel L as he left the locker room always pumped him up.

Then again, hockey *was* the land of F-bombs, so he wasn't sure he *could* call it channeling the famous Mr. Samuel L Jackson.

Regardless, Max was jazzed as he strode down the tunnel that led to the arena.

The crowds screamed as they headed for the bench—Max wasn't starting that night, and only the five players who'd be on the ice for puck drop stood at the blue line, gazes on the flags as they listened to the National Anthem.

He was Canadian born, so it wasn't quite the same as listening to "O Canada"—which was only sung when they played teams from the Frozen North—but it was still pretty awesome. Especially when the crowd got ramped up during the chorus and screamed so loudly at the end that his ears rang.

So. Fucking. Amazing.

Somehow, *this* was his life.

Somehow, he got to do his favorite thing for a living.

And he never *ever* forgot that he was one of the lucky ones. Yes, he worked hard. Yes, he busted his ass before and during the season. Hell yes, he played through injuries and colds and sore muscles.

But he got to play hockey.

And, Brayden aside, that was the best gift in his life.

Once the middle-aged man finished with the anthem and

the crew rolled up the carpet, Max and the rest of the players who weren't starting settled into place on the bench. There was an order, a rotation that made it easier for the players to swap positions, since hockey changes were typically on the fly. Those going on next sat closer to the doors, defense on the side closer to their goal and forwards on the other.

The ref blew his whistle and the centers squared off then . . . puck drop.

Both teams exploded into motion.

Blue won the puck back to their captain, Stefan—who also happened to be Brit's fiancé. They were sickeningly happy and way too lovey-dovey, especially considering they'd now been together a couple of years.

Wasn't that shit supposed to calm down after a while?

It certainly had been that way with him and his ex.

But also, Suzanne was a mega bitch, so . . . details.

Gold-induced happy endings or not—because the team had a hell of a track record, first with Brit and Stefan, then with his other teammates, Mike and Blane finding love—it was time to focus on the game.

Not on his ex. Not on all the shit that should have been.

This was time for self-discipline and for keeping the cylindrical black thingy out of their goal and strictly in the Canucks'.

They managed to get the puck into the offensive end, setting up and getting a shot on net before the Canucks' goalie covered the puck and the ref blew the whistle.

Then it was Max's turn to play.

He jumped onto the ice and lined up for the face-off. His mind worked in short staccato thoughts. Make a pass. Shoot. Deflected wide. Skate back to protect Brit and their net. Thirty-ish seconds passed before he hopped off the ice for a change.

The game continued that way.

Back and forth, hustling like a lunatic, hitting the other players, avoiding getting creamed himself for the most part, and by the time it was over, they'd managed to score two goals and the Canucks only one.

Yes.

Only fifty-eight more games to go in the season.

He snorted, wiping sweat from his brows as he completed a post-game interview before showering and heading to the PT suite to cool down and stretch.

Max was later than his normal time, so the facility was pretty much empty, and he had all the intentions of getting what he needed to get done and then GTFO-ing out. At least until he saw Mandy, their sports medicine guru and basically the reason the team was any form of healthy during the season, stow her supplies, pull her phone out of her pocket, and tap on the screen a few times.

He'd just started to turn toward the weight room when he saw her face fall.

Aw shit.

He glanced around for Blane before remembering his teammate had been pulled into Bernard's—their coach's—office.

Max might have still headed to cool down, to leave her to her privacy and not intrude, if he hadn't seen Mandy reach up and surreptitiously wipe one eye.

Fuck. She was family and she was sad and—

She was crying.

And he wasn't the type of guy who could leave a crying woman without at least making sure that she was all right. Sorry. He knew it was probably sexist, and nosy, but . . . Max just couldn't leave her.

"Hey," he murmured, crossing over to Mandy and snagging her arm. "Do you have a second?"

She sniffed, but her expression warmed. "Of course, Max. What's hurting?"

He tilted his head in the direction of her office. "Can we—?"

"Oh." Wide brown eyes. "Sure." She led the way, closing the door behind him, before turning her concerned gaze back to him. "Is everything okay? Is Brayden—?"

His heart squeezed in his chest, because, fuck, she was the best.

Mandy's job was the players' bodies, to keep them healthy and producing on the ice, but she knew they couldn't play to their full potential if their lives outside of the team had gone to shit. So, she'd also made it her priority to understand each detail of their lives away the rink, physical, family, or otherwise.

She'd even kept an eye on Brayden once when Max had promised to bring his son to a game and Anna, who'd planned on supervising, had fallen sick.

So yeah, he couldn't just breeze by and continue on with his night.

"We're fine," he said. "I'm more worried about you and why you're crying."

"I—"

He caught her hand, gave it a light squeeze, and gentled his voice. "I saw, sweetheart."

The endearment wasn't PC, but at least it seemed to get through because Mandy's eyes welled with tears. "I'm fine. Really," she hurried to add when he started to protest. "I just—I emailed my sister again and I haven't heard back and I'm hormonal and emotional and—"

Well, there was a lot to unpack in that statement, starting by asking, "Hormonal?" with one raised brow.

That was a specific word, reserved for only two specific situations.

And considering she hadn't mentioned cramps or mood swings, he felt safe in assuming exactly what kind of hormonal Mandy meant.

Which was the type that resulted in little people with shared DNA.

Her draw dropped. "Shit. I didn't mean to say that"—she lifted a finger, jabbing it in his face—"Not. One. Word. I just found out tonight, and I haven't even told Blane yet."

He lifted his palms up in surrender. "I'm a vault."

Her lids narrowed. "Good."

"So, your sister?"

Max found himself holding his breath, remembering his run-in with Mandy's sister. He'd told her, of course, had returned the printout of the email Angelica Shallows had inadvertently dropped in the hallway outside this very part of the Gold Mine.

He'd returned the email, but it hadn't been so easy to get Mandy's sister out of his brain.

Angelica.

Angel.

Sexy curves, porcelain skin, and warm brown eyes.

His dick had twitched upon first glance, and *that* hadn't happened in what felt like years.

But though Angelica Shallows might be beautiful, she'd also been running scared.

She'd apologized for intruding on the moment when Mandy and Blane had gotten engaged, panicked that her surprise appearance had ruined something precious. But what she hadn't realized, and what he hadn't gotten the chance to communicate was that as Mandy's sister, Angelica would have been welcomed with open arms.

They loved Mandy, and that meant Angelica had built-in street cred.

Unfortunately, Angelica hadn't stuck around to discover that.

And Max was *stuck* with the image of her worried face.

He'd thought about emailing her a dozen times.

Yet he'd resisted. He needed to focus on Brayden and stabilizing their lives, creating routine, and bonding with his son after a tumultuous few years. Not on rescuing or reassuring or hell, getting mixed up with a woman.

Not with *his* track record.

Mandy sniffed, jarring him from his thoughts enough that Max managed to pull his head out of his ass for half a second. "I emailed her again." She forced a smile. "I just found out I was pregnant, and I wanted to tell someone, and I thought . . . I guess I was just hoping that she might—" A shrug as she broke off.

"It's only been a couple of hours."

She nodded. "I know. So, I also know I'm being ridiculous."

Max bumped her shoulder with his. "Doesn't make it any easier though, does it?"

Mandy winced. "No." Her sigh was legit. "Ugh. Don't worry about me. I'm fine."

He slipped an arm around her waist, tugged her in for a hug. "You're *always* fine."

A grin. "Damn right, I am." Those lips fell. "But Max?"

"Yeah?"

"I'd really hoped this time would be different."

He gave her a gentle squeeze. "I know."

She'd just rested her head down on his shoulder when the office door opened, and Blane strode through. He took one look at them and glared, though Max knew him well enough to see he wasn't really annoyed. That fact was further confirmed by the gentleness of his tone. "Sweetheart? What's the matter?"

Mandy's face crumpled, Blane rushed over to take her in his arms, and Max used that quiet moment to slip out from the office.

But once again, Mandy's sister didn't slip so easily from his mind.

SIX

Angie

MONDAY MORNING BROUGHT LESS CODING and more managing, namely in the frustrating form of one of her most notorious troublemakers, Bailey.

Bailey was a fifty-something man who'd been with the company for years. And while he was a thorn in Angie's side, he'd worked at the company since before Heather had bought it and turned InDTech into RoboTech. But though he was experienced and a brilliant engineer, he also didn't take direction well, had horrible people skills, and frankly, tiptoed along the border of sexual harassment on a daily basis. All of which meant that if he'd been a normal employee Angie had hired, he would have been shit-canned week one.

But she hadn't hired him, and as an older person, he was a protected class of employee.

Basically, he could come back and sue them for age discrimination if he were let go without just cause.

And, unfortunately, just being an asshole wasn't just cause.

So, until Bailey did something outright—

She sighed and stopped dancing around the issue. Until he sexually harassed someone . . .

God, that sounded horrible. True, but still horrible.

But until Bailey did something egregious like that, or until he failed to do assignments enough times or didn't come to work on a regular basis or pulled out a stapler and tried to beat her over the head with it . . . well, the point was he needed to give her something so she could fire him.

Angie *had* been compiling a record of infractions on him, but none were enough to get him out of her hair.

Until that morning.

When he'd groped an employee under her skirt.

There had been a few incidents like this—one of Angie's employees feeling something, but not quite sure if it had been an actual grope or just accidental contact. Still, Bailey had always been smart in skating that line, or at least at pretending innocence.

But that morning Heather O'Keith saw the grope happen.

And that was how Angie found herself sitting in Heather's office, a very intimidating lawyer next to her in the receiving chairs, and her file of Bailey's incidents in her hand.

"What kind of grown man is named Bailey, anyway?" asked the lawyer, whom Heather had introduced as Rebecca Darden. She flipped through the pages as she spoke, and considering that her next sentence trailed quite rapidly after the first, there wasn't time, opportunity, or expectation for Angie to reply. "This is quite good." She glanced up and nodded approvingly at Angie. "Pair this with Heather's eyewitness account and the police report, and you should be able to get rid of him without issue."

"A severance?" Heather asked. "I hate to ask it since clearly, he's a scumbag, but that might be cheaper considering how expensive you are, Bec."

Bec sighed. "It's probably the least messy option." A shrug. "And cheaper. I can draft up a release so that he can't sue you or Angelica or the company in the future."

Angie's heart stopped for a second.

One because she hadn't even considered there was a risk of Bailey taking legal action against her. She certainly didn't have the connections that Heather did—no famous lawyer friends—and Angie, while she knew the company would protect her, knew Bailey was just vindictive enough to sue her, if only to make her life miserable.

Two, she was all too aware of the binding legal document, of the release she'd signed at eighteen.

A contract that prohibited her from making contact with Mandy.

One that stated, if she did contact Mandy or Mandy's mother, she would forfeit both hers and her own mother's inheritance.

Of course, her old man was dead now, her mother gone as well, so that threat held little power. Plus, she'd never even spent the money from her dad. It had always felt icky to her, layered with lies and deceit and way too fucking much manipulation.

So, for the hundredth time in the past six months, she went around and around and around.

Could she chance it?

Maybe?

But what if she ruined Mandy's life? Brought drama and unease and—

No. That wasn't it either. Or not *all* of it, anyway.

Because the real piece of this fucked up puzzle, the major thing that was holding Angie back was . . .

What if she got hurt?

What if she opened her heart and let Mandy in and then got hurt?

Yeah.

That.

Angie sighed internally. She was a chicken. A giant, pathetic chicken.

Bec stood, grabbing her bag and jarring Angie out of her reverie. She nodded at Heather. "Give me a couple of hours, and I'll have something airtight for you." She shook Angie's hand. "Good job being meticulous. This wouldn't have been as easy if you hadn't been."

The door closed quietly behind her.

Angie pushed to her feet. "I'm going to check on Kristin"— the woman Bailey had groped and who was still in with the detective from the police department—"make sure she doesn't need anything."

"Absolutely," Heather said. "But I need you to give me another minute of your time."

Oh, fuck.

Stomach sinking, Angie plunked down into the chair.

"You're not in trouble." Heather's lips twitched. "I'm flying out tomorrow and wanted to check in with you about Kelsey and Sebastian."

Angie frowned. "Um. They're both fine. Been a real pleasure to work with, actually."

Heather nodded. "I'm glad to hear that. Sometimes brother-sister working relationships can be challenging." A self-deprecating grin, considering she worked with her own brother.

But that wasn't what she was talking about, was it? Angie struggled to process the undertones of that statement, because she didn't think Heather was referring to her own brother Jordan, but the fact that Kelsey and Sebastian were related.

Her brows pulled tighter. "I-uh . . . what?"

Could they be related? And if so, why had neither of them said anything?

She met her boss's gaze, the question no doubt written across her face.

Heather inclined her head.

Holy shit. "I had no idea they were brother and sister," Angie said softly. "They work well together, and I've never seen a single squabble over . . . well, I'm an only child"—she ignored the pang in her heart—"so whatever it is that siblings fight over."

"Hmm," Heather said before her lips curved. "I swear that half the time Jordan forgets that I'm the boss now. We argue about that more than anything."

Angie relaxed. "No way. He loves passing along the tough jobs to you."

"Maybe," Heather replied. "But regardless, I'm glad that the Scott crew is behaving itself. Let me know if any issues arise that you can't handle."

"I'll try to make it so it's not police reports and firings."

Heather's cell rang. "I'd appreciate that," she said before answering the call.

Angie excused herself, closing the door quietly behind herself then going to check in on Kristin. The police were still taking her statement, so Angie returned with the requested bottles of water and left them to finish.

She'd just sat down at her desk and was checking her email when the message came through.

Her heart stopped.

Her palms instantly went sweaty.

Her thighs squeezed together.

Because she recognized the name, and the moment she did so, she also remembered every single one of the feelings the man who that particular name belonged to had summoned within her.

Embarrassment. Fear. Then heat. So much heat that she'd turned tail and run.

Angie had never seen a man more beautiful that Max Montgomery.

Yes, she knew his name. Yes, she'd Googled the Gold's roster after her run-in with Max. Yes, she'd Googled *Max* after she'd Googled the team.

She was a Googling machine, and the results had. Been. Glorious.

Max was sexy as shit and model gorgeous. Even the little bump on his nose signaling that body part having been broken a time or two was perfectly centered and added to his attraction rather than detracting from it.

The man should be on the Silver Screen, not skating circles on the ice.

Okay, so he did more than just skate circles—and Angie had to admit she knew this because she'd watched the Gold play with scary regularity since meeting Max. He was a talented player, with occasional glimpses of brilliance, and she had seen the Gold's coach put him on the ice more than once when he needed someone steady to calm the team.

So yeah, Max Montgomery was successful, hot, and good at his job.

His eyes had also held interest, and he'd called her Angel.

"Dangerous," she whispered.

But she clicked to open it anyway.

What she read in the email made her morning look like it had been filled with rainbows and puppy dogs rather than groping and police reports.

Fuck. Her. Life.

SEVEN

Max

HE'D DOUBLE-CHECKED his alarm this time.

He had.

He'd looked at his phone just before tumbling headfirst into bed and made sure his alarm was set and ready to go . . . for the morning this time.

"Fuck," he muttered, lurching up in bed after seeing the screen of his cell.

8:17.

A.M.

Fuck.

Brayden's school had started seventeen minutes ago. He was incompetent and useless and—

He could save the mental bashing for a later time.

For now, they needed to haul ass.

Max jumped out of bed and sprinted for his closet, throwing on a T-shirt and a pair of sweats before shoving his feet into sneakers. Then he ran down the hall to wake up Brayden.

But before he had actually opened the door to his son's room, he happened to glance back down at his phone.

And saw it was Saturday.

As in not a school day.

As in he could have still been sleeping.

Max groaned and quietly made his way back down the hall. Brayden's room had remained silent during his shenanigans, so luckily his sprinting hadn't woken his son or Sparky, who'd come home with them that day two weeks before and had quickly fit right into their lives.

Max hadn't had any success in changing Sparky's name—Brayden thought it was "absolutely perfect" and "could they please, *please* keep it?" and after a statement like that from a seven-year-old boy, how could a father deny his son such a small request?

He couldn't.

Sparky it was.

The best part of the entire adoption process—besides the fact that Sparky was an awesome pooch and Max already couldn't imagine their life without him—was that Anna had been *absolutely perfect* in her selection.

Sparky was chill, sweet, and had been beyond great with Brayden, so much so that Sparky's permanent crate was now in Brayden's room.

Hence, Max tiptoeing back to his bedroom so he didn't wake beast or boy.

He sighed, toeing off his shoes before flopping onto the mattress and closing his eyes. Unfortunately, the underside of his lids did not bring back peaceful oblivion.

"Fuck," he grumbled and pushed back out of bed.

Despite the four hours of sleep, he was officially up. Panic and a hallway sprint would do that to a man. *Fuck.* At this point, he might as well shower and make breakfast.

Max was halfway through soaping up when Brayden and Sparky burst into the bathroom.

"Dad!" Brayden said, one hand over his mouth. His words were partially muffled. "Sparky threw up. It smells *horrible.*"

Max froze, suds sliding down his body. This was karma. Had to be.

He'd successfully avoided the mom talk and in return?

Vomit.

He hung up the loofa and hurried to rinse off. "Take him outside, bud, in case he pukes a—"

Sparky upchucked on the bath mat.

"—gain."

"*Ew!*" Brayden retched.

"Out!" Max ordered, wanting to get his son out of the splash zone before he had two sources of puke to clean up. "Get dressed."

Brayden nodded, turned to leave.

"Close the door behind you," he called before Sparky followed him out and trailed vomit through the house.

Brayden moved at Flash-speed, slamming the door closed, and leaving Max trapped with the vomit monster.

He quickly rinsed the shampoo from his hair then wrenched the water off, grabbing his towel and wrapping it around his hips before stepping out, careful to avoid the soiled mat. In the meantime, Sparky barfed again, this time on Max's sweats, which he'd left in the corner of the room when he'd undressed for the shower.

Anna would say he should have put them away in the first place.

Then again, she'd also said Sparky would be the perfect pooch for them.

"Perfect," he grumbled. "*Ha.* Not so much." But he knelt next to Sparky until he'd finished then scratched the obviously miserable dog behind his ears. "I'm sorry, buddy. We'll get you some help."

Max stood, sidestepped the puddles, and hurried into the closet to get dressed, round two. After tugging on fresh sweats and a shirt, he grabbed his cell and called the vet while tugging on his shoes. Thankfully, they were open, and he made arrangements to bring Sparky in immediately. Then he threw a couple of towels over his shoulder—he didn't want barf splatter-painting the back of his SUV—scooped up the pooch and fumbled to open the bathroom door.

Brayden barged through at the same moment and only quick reflexes stopped Max from getting a doorknob in the face.

How he would have explained that one to the team . . .

Brayden immediately slapped a hand over his mouth and retched again.

"Car," Max said. "We're taking Sparky to the vet."

To his son's credit, Brayden didn't spend a second arguing. Instead, he whirled and ran for the stairs.

It wasn't until they were in the waiting room at the vet's office, the staff having taken Sparky into the back, that Max saw the first sign of worry.

"I-is Sparky going to be okay?"

"The vet is going to help him feel better," he said instead of promising that. Sparky had vomited at least a half-dozen more times on the fifteen-minute drive and had been very lethargic when Max had carried him in. He wasn't sure what that meant. Was it a stomach bug? Did dogs *even* get stomach bugs? Or—

Hell, he didn't know.

The door opened, and Anna rushed through. Her hair was slicked back into a ponytail, her eyes wild, and her face pale. She saw them and hurried over. "Oh my God, are you guys okay? Is Sparky—"

"He's with the vet," Max told her. "They're trying to figure out what's up with him."

"Oh," she said, voice small. "I'm—" She sniffed and shook her head. "Sorry," she croaked out, clearly panicked but trying to hold it together for Brayden.

Max felt bad for calling her. He'd try to play it cool, to make her see that she . . . "I-I love him." A breath, her tone more normal. "I'm just a little worried."

Brayden moved before Max could, wrapping his little arms around her waist. "It'll be okay," he said. "Dad says the vet will make Sparky feel better."

Anna nodded, squeezed him back. "You're right, of course. *Both* of you."

"Can you stay here with him for a little bit?" Max asked after Brayden had wandered off to play with some toys on the other side of the lobby. "I want to go home and clean up."

Anna frowned. "Clean up?"

Max shrugged. "Sparky attempted to redecorate the house."

"Ew." Anna made a face just as the front door opened. Out of the corner of his eye, Max saw a flash of dark hair, the outline of a cat carrier. "I can go clean it up."

"No," he argued. "It's a *mess*, Anna. You don't want—"

"Messes I can deal with," she said, lifting one shoulder. "And I'm an old hand at puke."

"It's a *lot* of puke and not your job—"

"Whose idea was it to get Sparky, hmm?"

He raised a brow. "Mine."

Anna huffed. "That's not what I meant. I picked him, and —" She sniffed. "*Ugh*," she groaned. "Why am I so emotional about a dog?"

"Because the little asshole has grown on us?"

Her jaw dropped, but then she gave a little giggle. Max slid an arm around her shoulders and tugged her in for a hug. "It'll be fine."

"Good. So, you stay because I'm too emotional to make doggy decisions and I'd rather go back to your house and clean up puke."

He released her. "You sure?"

A nod. "Absolutely."

"Good." He grinned. "Then you can start with the back of my car."

She rolled her eyes, smacked him across the chest, but snagged his keys. "I'll be back," she told him. "With a clean car. But just so you know, you now owe me tickets for the next game against the Rangers. I'm going to root for them." She pretended to glare. "Loudly."

"You're evil."

One blond brow lifted. "Do we have a deal?"

Max snorted. "Yes, we have a deal."

She nodded, waving and heading for the door. Just before she pushed through, Max happened to glance over at Brayden and saw who his son was talking to.

"What the—?"

EIGHT

Angie

ANGIE LOOKED DOWN at the sweet little boy. He was staring up at her with bright blue eyes, though his expression was serious.

"Is your cat sick, too?" he asked, eyeing the carrier in her hand.

"No," she said. "Sammy's just here for a checkup. Want to take a peek?"

He nodded, and she set the carrier on a chair so the boy could look in. "He's a little unhappy being cooped up but just fine. Do you do checkups with your doctor?"

He nodded again. "Dr. Lexington. He's nice."

"So's the vet here."

He poked a finger through one hole in the carrier, and she heard Sammy start purring. She'd lucked out with her kitty—he was sweet, calm, and loved people.

And kids, too, apparently, because the little boy extracted his finger with an expression of pure joy. "He kissed me!"

Angie bent to look in at Sammy.

Her kitty was purring up a storm and rubbing against the sides of her cage. "He likes you."

"Really?"

She nodded. "Really. My name's Angie, what's yours?"

"Brayden."

"Well, it's very nice to meet you, Brayden."

"Want to introduce me to your friend?"

Angie froze, a wave of heat sliding down her spine. She knew that voice, and it belonged to the man who'd sent her the email on Monday, the one that had caused her heart to fissure and crack, the one that she was still too damned cowardly to act on.

No.

She wasn't supposed to be thinking about that.

She was *supposed* to be focusing on work, on filling the hole left from Bailey's rapid and abrupt departure.

She couldn't be thinking about Max or her sister or the fact that her cowardice was probably preventing her from experiencing a lot in this world.

Hell, Angie *had* just put herself out there by spending time with Kelsey and the girls. That had been decidedly out of her comfort zone, and she . . . had almost run that night.

Ugh, brain, she thought.

Because that was definitely not what she should be focused on.

She was making progress.

Yes, she was isolated. Yes, it was hard for her to get out there and do new things, but her job as a manager meant that she now dealt with people on a daily basis and that in and of itself was a huge improvement from where she'd been when her mom had died.

It's not enough.

No, it wasn't.

But, marathon not sprint. She needed to remember that.

"This is Angie," Brayden said. "She has a cat. His name is Sammy, and he licked my finger." Brayden made a face. "It felt kind of weird, but I liked it."

And if that wasn't an allegory for Angie's life, then she didn't know what was.

"Hi, Angie," Max said softly.

"Hi."

Silence. Brayden resuming his appraisal of Sammy, and Angie studying the whiteness of her shoelaces.

Fingers under her chin made her flinch and step back.

"Don't touch," she said, gaze still glued on the floor.

She couldn't get through this if he touched her.

Max put his hands up, increased the distance between them. "I'm sorry."

Brayden chose that moment to grab her arm. "Sammy kissed me again." She found herself ruffling his hair with her free hand.

Kids were okay. Women were okay.

Men were . . . problematic.

As though they were opposite poles on a magnet, her eyes slipped from Brayden and Sammy up to Max.

His expression was intense, a sliver of fury in his gaze.

"It's men," she found herself blurting. "Well, that's not it. It's more complicated than that . . . Ever since—" Angie caught herself just in time, tearing her gaze from his, focusing back on the much safer topic of Brayden. "He's a darling little boy," she said. "You and your wife must be thrilled."

Max was silent for a moment then, "I'm not married." A pause. "Ever since what?"

She ignored the question. "Oh, I'm sorry. I saw your girl-friend leave and just assumed. I shouldn't—"

"My nanny," he said quietly. "Ever since what?" he repeated.

Her and her big mouth. But now what? She'd been to a lot of therapy, had filed a police report, had gone to trial and testified. All of that had almost been easier than moving on with her life.

Especially since the perpetrator was still in jail. She *should* be able to move on. It was just . . . well, she'd been permanently changed. Ten minutes had intrinsically altered the course of her life. She *still* struggled with touch, and with male touch in particular. Though, she'd gotten to the point now that if she initiated contact, then she was fine. But if *they* did, then she struggled to not be drawn back into those dark memories.

Angie just needed to remember she *was* getting better. Hell, she'd even gone on a couple of dates. Been kissed a time or two since.

But it didn't change the fact that she'd been transformed.

And not for the better.

An isolated girl, newly orphaned and totally alone in the world. Beyond naïve.

Prime pickings for a predator who'd been interested in raping a very inexperienced young woman.

But though she still grappled with anxiety, even six years later—the attack having made her already nervous nature worse —the single thing Angie had never grappled with was shame.

The assault was not her fault.

"I was attacked," she said, lifting her chin.

"Hurt?" Max's eyes blazed now, and Angie found she couldn't look away.

"Yes."

His gaze flicked to Brayden then back to meet hers. "In *that* way?"

Appreciating that he wanted to protect his son, Angie just nodded. "Years ago now, but some patterns are hard to break."

"I'm sorry," he said.

A shrug. "Me, too."

"I'm going—" He shook his head. "Is it okay if I touch you?"

Every nerve in Angie's body froze. "I—uh—" *No*, her mind said.

But . . . then for some reason she wouldn't be able to explain or understand even later, she nodded.

It made no logical sense that it was okay for Max to touch her when contact from other men made her uncomfortable—Max was huge and visibly strong. He towered over her, could hurt her easily, but in some deep, secret place in Angie's heart, she trusted him to *not* hurt her. And, if she was being completely honest, she *wanted* his touch, ached to see what it felt like.

Slowly, so *slowly*, Max reached a hand toward her.

His thumb had just brushed her chin when—

"Sammy?"

Angie jumped back, grabbed Sammy's carrier with an apology to Brayden, and flicked an unsure gaze toward Max. "Uh, sorry. I need to—"

"Angel?" he asked softly.

"Yeah?"

"My email." His voice was careful. "Did you read it?"

She nodded.

He looked at her expectantly and . . . she just couldn't do it.

Pathetic, but there it was.

The shake of her head came after he'd already read the truth on her face. "It's ok—"

"It's not," Angie interjected. "It's really not, but I still can't."

She couldn't bring her baggage into her sister's life. Not now, not when Mandy was happy and going to have a baby.

This was Mandy's chance for a future, and Angie couldn't bring her down.

Which sounded really noble and it might even *have* been if not for that fact that the real reason she hadn't reached out to Mandy was because deep down she was scared to try.

Ugh.

With a sigh, she hurried after the vet tech.

Inside the room, Sammy's appointment was quick and uneventful. Then Angie was walking back down the hall and out into the lobby all the while unsure if she was actually anticipating seeing Max again or just petrified to potentially be back in front of a man she didn't really know but somehow had revealed so much to.

In the end, it turned out she didn't need to worry about either of those.

When she emerged into the front of the vet's office, there was no sign of Brayden or Max.

Disappointed.

She wasn't disappointed.

Aw hell. She was.

"JUST YOU AND ME, SAM," Angie murmured, pushing through the door to her apartment and setting Sammy's carrier on the floor.

She used her heel to close the door before opening Sammy's cage, having spent too many times chasing her kitty down the halls. He never seemed to want to *really* escape, but he did have a great time leading her on a merry chase outside her neighbors' doors.

Sammy slid from the carrier and began twining around her ankles.

It was early Saturday, and she had the whole day—hell, the whole *weekend*—ahead of her.

No plans.

Lame.

Maybe she'd reorganize her sock collection? Currently, she had them ordered alphabetically by movie title, but maybe she should group them by genre?

"Oh, my God," she groaned.

Was she seriously considering grouping her socks by genre?

That was a hundred times worse than having no plans.

Maybe she should go out, walk around the city. There was a new art exhibit at the de Young that looked really interesting. Except . . . just the thought of going somewhere she hadn't planned for, somewhere she'd only been to once before, was terrifying. The vet was one thing—Angie had spent years getting comfortable with taking Sammy there, and plus he *needed* to go. She wouldn't put an innocent creature at risk just because she was scared.

But dammit, she hadn't gone to years of therapy, working through the attack, her childhood, to *not* do something she wanted.

Fuck fear. She was going and that was the end of it.

So there.

"And who am I trying to convince, huh?" she muttered, stashing the carrier in her hall closet and storming into her bedroom. "Why am I still like this? Why do I hide in fiction when I want to live?" She paused in front of her mirror, staring at her reflection. A pretty face, nice skin, pale brown eyes, and what books would describe as kissable lips.

She'd enjoyed kissing once. It had been an escape, a way to get lost in feelings that were pleasurable instead of terrifying.

Until the attack had made her a writhing ball of nerves.

Until every date she'd forced herself to go on since then had been a disaster.

Even if she did manage to get to the kissing stage, she felt . . . nothing.

Until Max.

One look, and she'd *felt*. One touch, and her skin had been on fire. One email, and he'd punched a giant hole in her barriers—

Enough.

Because truthfully, she'd lowered her barriers the moment Mandy had reached out.

That was why—

"I'm going to that fucking art exhibit. And I'm going now."

Her expression was grim but determined.

"Fuck all this fear shit. I want to live."

NINE

Max

SPARKY WAS able to come home after a few hours at the vet. He'd received something called subcutaneous fluids, which basically meant he had a hump of liquids under the skin between his shoulder blades that could rival Quasimodo. It wobbled and jiggled with every step he took, poor guy.

But he was medicated, on a prescribed bland diet, and most importantly, Sparky was no longer puking.

Turned out their adopted pooch had Irritable Bowel Syndrome—he hadn't even known dogs could *get* IBS—and the special chew treat Max and Brayden had given him the night before in his crate at bedtime had caused the poltergeist of puking this morning.

The vet had told them he was lucky that it hadn't been the other way.

And Max was more than inclined to believe her.

Anna had cleaned the house and his car before coming back to pick up Brayden from the vet's office, so he wasn't cooped up while Sparky was being treated. They'd gone to the park, eaten ice cream, visited the library . . . basically Anna had pulled out all the stops in order to distract him.

Eventually, the vet had asked Max to go back into an exam room and explained what was going on. After the vet's debriefing, Max had passed on the news to his little minions and so Brayden and Anna had made one final stop at the pet store for a new cushy bed and what looked like a hundred new toys, if his living room was any indication.

"Come here, Sparky," Brayden said, coaxing the pup over to his new bed. He sank down on the floor and began scratching behind the dog's ears. "Are you feeling better?"

Sparky rolled over to his side and soaked up the attention.

"I'm ready with all his new food and wrote up a strict diet plan," Anna began.

Max squeezed her shoulders and guided her to the front door. "No game tonight," he reminded. "This is your chance to go out and party hard like the young'un you are."

Anna snorted. "I'll be back tomorrow around ten to watch the boys."

"Thanks, Anna," he said. "You're the best."

A smile. "That I know."

"Here." He handed her a couple of bills. "For your overtime today and to reimburse you for all the cleaning."

"Max, this is way too much—"

"Hush," he told her. "Enjoy your Saturday."

She shook her head at him but pocketed the money and waved. "See you tomorrow."

"Movie night?" Max asked once the front door had closed.

"Yes!" Brayden fist-pumped. "We're on *Empire Strikes Back*! I need to find out what happens with Luke."

"I'll make popcorn, you get the blankets and pillows. I think we should watch down here with Sparky, don't you?"

Brayden barely nodded before sprinting up the stairs.

By the time he was back with the popcorn and drinks, Brayden had the king of all blanket forts set up, Sparky was passed out on his new bed, and the movie was cued up on the TV.

He handed Brayden a bowl, pressed play, and felt his heart melt all over again when his son snuggled close.

God. He loved his kid.

POST-GAME AFTER A LOSS was never fun, but some of the guys from the team had made dinner plans in order to celebrate Blane and Mandy's pregnancy, so they all compartmentalized that away and focused on the fact that Blane was about to be a dad.

"He's totally going to lose it when he has to change a diaper," Brit teased, as they all settled into chairs around a large table in a private room. They were at their favorite burger place, complete with campy decorations and red velvet drapes.

The burgers were loads better than the décor.

"Am not," Blane retorted.

"Are too," she countered, a smile tugging up the corners of her mouth.

She and Blane had grown up together, the latter having a crush on the former for many years, but when Brit had started seeing Stefan several seasons ago, Blane had spent some time reevaluating his life. Eventually, he'd paired up with Mandy and now they were ridiculously happy.

"Diapers aren't going to do him in," Stefan added. "He's going to pass out in the delivery room."

Mandy scowled. "No talk of delivery rooms. I've blocked that part out."

Brit lifted her glass, tapping it with Mandy's. "I would too, dude. I would, too."

Max almost said, *"It's not so bad,"* but luckily, he caught himself just in time. That particular sentiment would earn him no favors at this table. And rightfully so. It hadn't been bad . . . for *him*. But he'd done the easy lifting, ending up with the best kid anyone could ask for.

"As the only one with a kid who's currently sitting at this table," he said, "I can say they are worth all the angst and worry and pain. Your heart . . . it just . . . expands somehow when they come into your life."

Mike grinned. "That's deep."

Sara, his wife and a former champion figure skater, smacked him across the chest. "Stop it, you."

Stefan rolled his eyes. "Brayden seems to have settled in. This season is better than last?"

"Yes," Max said. "Anna has made all the difference. Total lifesaver. How did you find her again?"

"She was the girl who helped my mom when she was sick the first time in Minnesota"—Stefan's mom had fought and beat cancer twice—"When I heard she'd moved to California, I knew she would be awesome for you and Brayden."

Max topped off his beer. "Thank you. I literally don't know how I would do it without her."

He'd nearly lost his mind before Anna. He'd already worried about Brayden while he was on the road with Suzanne not in the picture, but unreliable babysitters and a string of nannies who'd wanted to be *more* than nannies, hadn't helped matters.

Thanks to Suzanne, his reputation had preceded him.

Unfortunately for the nannies, his reputation wasn't true. He didn't diddle with the staff, hadn't cheated on his wife, and he sure as hell wasn't the father to anyone aside from Brayden.

As the DNA test had proven.

But while the media tended to be *really* good at getting a scandal out there, they weren't so great at spreading the news of retractions.

He got it.

The juicy bits were way more fun to read than boring legalese.

It had just been easier when those juicy bits weren't about him.

" . . . since we're all here, Mike and I . . . well, we have something to tell you, too." Max tuned back into the conversation right as Sara finished her soft statement. "I don't want to take anything away from your special night," she continued. "But Mike and I—"

Brit squealed. Yes, the tough, super fit, first female player in the NHL clapped her hands together as she released a high-pitched squeal. "You're pregnant!"

Sara nodded.

There were hugs and congratulations and fist bumps all around, and by the time they had all settled themselves back into their chairs, their entrees had arrived. Just as they dug in, Brit tapped her fork to her glass.

They all glanced up at her. She peeked over at Stefan, her lips curving. "Just since we're on the topic of news . . . Stefan and I—"

"Oh fuck," Blue, the only other single man at the table, said. "You're not pregnant, too? What about our season?"

Max took it upon himself to smack Blue on the back of the head. "Dude."

"What?" he asked, rubbing at the spot.

Brit rolled her eyes at him. "I'm not pregnant. We have this funny thing nowadays called birth control. Super effective, Blue. You should look into it."

"Ew," Mandy said.

"Hey. Shut it, you. You're supposed to be a medical professional," Brit countered, pointing a finger at her. "Plus, I got that shit locked up tight. No swimmers making themselves at home in my uterus until we're ready."

Max blinked. "Okay then."

Blane smirked. "What was your news, Brit?"

She held up her hand, and Max saw she was wearing a second silicone ring. One was glittery pink and the other pale white, because while Brit might be tough and talented, she could and *did* embrace her feminine side—damn all the haters saying she was too weak and female to play hockey or on the inverse that she was too masculine to still be considered a woman.

Brit found her own way and she always had.

"Stefan and I eloped!" she said.

And so more congratulations erupted, followed by more hugs and fist bumps, until they made such a ruckus their server came to check on them.

Their burgers were lukewarm by the time they finally settled down to eat.

Being surrounded by his friends, his *family,* meant they tasted as good as ever.

Despite losing the game, it was a great night.

Because over the last few seasons, Max had learned that hockey wasn't everything.

Family was more important.

TEN

Angie

OKAY, she was doing this. She could *totally* do this.

Blowing out a few breaths like she was a prizefighter readying herself to enter the ring, Angie pressed the call button on her cell.

It rang once before the panic took over and she ended the call.

"Dammit," she hissed, throwing her phone onto the couch. "*Come on.* You can do this. You just need to suck it up and—"

But before she could get herself good and psyched up for round two of attempted calling, her cell started ringing.

"Oh shit," she said, making a little panicked circle in her living room. "Oh shit, oh shit. Oh—"

She needed to answer the phone.

She grabbed it, swept a finger across the screen, and put it up to her ear.

"Hello?"

"Angie?" Kelsey said. "I answered your call, but there wasn't anyone there. Is everything okay?"

"Of course," she replied hastily. "I . . . um . . . was just driving through a tunnel and . . . uh . . . I guess the call dropped." Angie shrugged noncommittally, even though Kelsey couldn't see it.

"Okay."

Cue silence.

"What were you calling about?" Kelsey asked after a moment.

"Oh. Um. I just wanted to see if you wanted to grab lunch or dinner," Angie said. "Or maybe just a coffee? I'm open. I . . . uh—"

"Sure," Kelsey said. "I don't have any plans. What time is good for you?"

"Want to meet me in an hour or so?"

"Does that give you enough time?"

"Huh?"

"From wherever you're driving to."

"Oh." Angie sank onto her couch, dropped her forehead into her free hand. "For sure. I'm heading home now."

"Great. Do you know Dean's? Their omelets are *so* good." Kelsey chuckled. "I went to yoga this morning and was trying to be good, so I've only had this disgusting green protein shake thing, and I'm starving. They have killer brews of coffee, too."

The next words that came out of Angie's mouth would have been impossible several years before.

But she'd come a long way.

She just needed to remember that.

"I've never been," Angie said, "but I'm game to try somewhere new."

Of course, she'd Yelp the shit out of the restaurant beforehand, pick her top three menu items, research the brew types, and be totally ready to order so her anxiety wouldn't smother

her when she was sitting at the table and already forced to make one-on-one conversation.

Conversation.

One-on-one.

Oh shit, why was she doing this again?

"Awesome! I'll see you in an hour." Kelsey hung up, stopping Angie from blurting out an excuse to forget the whole thing. Perhaps she could get stuck in that fucking made up tunnel and not emerge until next year. Yeah, that could work.

But then her cell pinged with a text.

That almost-crippling panic chilled.

Kelsey had sent her a link to Dean's Yelp listing.

Damn, she was good.

ANGIE WAS JUST GIVING her name to the hostess when Kelsey walked in. "Hey," she said, after the girl had told them it would just be a couple of minutes. Her blond hair swung around her shoulders in soft waves, and she wore a warm smile on her lips.

"Hi," Angie said and tried not to freeze when Kelsey gave her a quick squeeze.

God, she was so out of practice with the friend thing.

"Oh no," Kelsey said, releasing her. "You're doing fine."

Angie groaned, realized she'd spoken the last statement verbally. "Don't you see? If I wasn't out of practice being a friend, I wouldn't have said that aloud."

"Hush. You're fine—"

"I can seat you now."

Kelsey smiled at the hostess and they followed her to a table. "So, why are you out of practice being a friend?" she asked after they were settled.

Angie sucked in a breath. "Well, my childhood wasn't conventional"—being the secret love child of a famous hockey player was hardly normal—"I was kept pretty isolated, homeschooled, and then I did the online college thing." She shrugged. "But after my mom died, I was alone in the world and I . . ." Her words trailed off.

"You don't have to tell me."

She shook her head, took a breath, and kept her gaze focused on the green-checked tablecloth. "I was assaulted and after that, all of my anxieties just amplified. It took me a few years to understand that I was in trouble and a few more in therapy to feel semi-normal again. And that's saying something for how far I've come because I'm really fucking weird still."

Kelsey frowned. "But you seem fine. I mean, I wouldn't have noticed anything if you hadn't said. I mean . . . we're scientists, engineers, and we come with our own special brands of socially awkward."

Angie snorted.

"But you manage the department so well. You're great with all of us, the number of different projects, finding a way to pivot between them. And how you handled the situation with Bailey." She shrugged. "I mean, you were so good, dude."

"Thanks," Angie murmured. "For whatever reason, work has always been fine for me." A shrug. "I mean, I guess it makes sense. It's my happy place, for sure." She unfolded her napkin, dropped it in her lap. "Plus, I've had a few years now to get used to managing. It's gotten easier."

Kelsey nodded. "Honestly, I just assumed you were shy."

Angie smiled. "I'll take that."

"Did they—" Kelsey broke off, picking up her menu and starting to look through it. "Never mind. That's too nosy. So, I always get the Denver omelet and the dark brew, but I don't think you can really go wrong here."

Angie used her finger to tip the menu down. "Isn't being nosy what friends do?"

Kelsey tilted her head to the side. "I guess."

"So, ask," Angie said. "It's okay."

"I was just wondering if they got the guy."

"*Oh.*" Angie blinked away the memories of that night—the rain, rough fingers tearing open her jeans, pain from her head colliding with pavement. "Yes. Luckily someone came and interrupted my attacker. He detained the guy until the police showed up."

"Wow."

"I was really lucky, all things considered. The guy is still in prison and will be for a long time. My attack wasn't his first rodeo."

"Holy shit, dude. That's crazy."

Angie picked up her menu, though she'd already memorized it beforehand. "I know. And that's not even the craziest. My childhood was—"

Kelsey clapped her hands together. "Oh my God. What? Are you a princess in disguise? A former child star? Maybe a fugitive on the run?"

Angie's jaw dropped open. "Uh . . . nope. None of those."

Kelsey pfted. "Damn. I was hoping for a good fiction trope." She clapped her hands together. "So, dish. What was it?"

"A story for another time, how about that?"

"Tease." Kelsey rolled her eyes, but her mouth was curved into a smile. "Does this story need a side dish of alcohol?"

"Definitely," Angie said. "Anyway." She waved her hand. "Tell me about—"

Their server came over, and they spent the next few minutes ordering drinks and food. After he'd gone, Kelsey started talking about an employee she'd dealt with at her previous employer, a company that had held several government contracts. But the employee made Bailey look like Santa Claus or the Tooth Fairy—meaning slightly creepy but with good intentions . . . and who may bring a present or a dollar as a byproduct.

Then Kelsey had Angie in stitches as she recited a few great blackmail stories from Sebastian's childhood, and finally near tears—of humor—when she described going to her first college party as a sixteen-year-old high school graduate and puking up her first taste of beer all over the cutest guy in the room.

"My ability to hold in my alcohol has improved since then," Kelsey said. "And despite giving it the good college try, I still can't stand the taste of Bud Light."

"But you're still a lightweight."

Kels smiled. "Cheap date. I prefer to think of it like that."

"Good point."

They finished eating, split the bill, and paused just outside the restaurant. "Thanks for inviting me out," Kelsey said. "I needed real food."

"That may have been the best omelet of my life, so thanks for the suggestion." A moment of awkward quiet. "Well, I'll see you tomorrow." She waved, started to turn for her car, but Kelsey stopped her with a hand on her shoulder.

"I think you're really brave. For pushing through the fear." A squeeze. "It's impressive, and I hope you know that."

Angie shook her head. "I'm such a mess. There are so many things I'm still scared of, things that I'm avoiding."

"We all avoid things. We're all scared." She lifted a hand. "I'm sorry, that sounded douchey and minimizing, I just meant that we're all a mess, and I think it's amazing you're trying to push through."

Angie tilted her chin up to the clouds, watched the fog move in misty tendrils as it turned the sky gray. "What if I *can't* push through? What if I'm always going to be like this?"

"You do what everyone else does. You struggle up one step at a time, until finally, eventually, *painfully*, you're at the top of the stairs."

Angie met Kelsey's gaze, saw earnestness in its depths. God, Angie really liked her. "Then what? You choose to go left or right?"

"Exactly. Or maybe you find yourself crawling up another staircase," she said. "And that's fucking fine, too. Because you're moving toward something rather than being stuck in stasis."

Angie's heart was pounding. "Life's too fucking short to be stuck in stasis."

"Exactly." Kelsey hugged her again and this time, Angie didn't have to force herself to do anything. She just hugged her friend back.

"You're pretty smart," she said. "I hope you know that."

"Occasionally, I get lucky," Kels told her with a grin. "Okay, we're both going to pick the thing that terrifies us the most and we're going to do it. Deal?"

Angie blinked at the sharp left the conversation took. "Uh . . ."

"Don't wimp out on me now," Kelsey said. "I'm going to go home, call my ex, and apologize for choosing a job over our relationship. What are you most afraid of?"

She shook her head. "I can't—"

Kelsey pulled out her cell and dialed a number. "Tanner? Hey, it's Kelsey. I was a total bitch and completely horrible to you. I've regretted how I handled things with you for years. I'm so, so sorry." She paused and listened. "I know. It doesn't change anything, but I did want to let you know that it's one of my biggest regrets, and I was wrong to—" She broke off, listened for a few more beats. "No, I'm not drunk. Just slightly more mature and human."

Angie listened to the one-sided conversation with wide eyes.

"Yes, exactly." A laugh. "I know we were young." Another pause. "The mistakes were more on my end than yours, let's face it." She laughed again. "Thanks, Tanner. If you're ever in San Francisco, we should grab a coffee. Mmm-hmm. Okay, bye!"

She hung up, and Angie just stared at her. "What is wrong with you?"

"I'm annoyingly impulsive and have a big mouth," Kelsey replied without missing a beat.

They looked at each for a heartbeat before exploding into laughter.

When they'd recovered enough to talk, Kelsey laced her arm through Angie's. "Okay, girlfriend. You're up. What are you most afraid of?"

Angie sucked in a breath, released it, and finally just told the truth.

"Email."

One email in particular, from a man who made her heart race.

Kelsey raised a brow. "What about email? Reading it? Replying to it? Being inundated with spam?"

She snorted. "Not spam," Angie said. "I just—I don't know what to say to him."

"Ah." Clarity danced across Kelsey's face. "My advice is to open the email and just start typing. And when you run out of things to say . . ."

"What?"

"Just hit send."

ELEVEN

Max

HE'D JUST FINISHED CHECKING in on Brayden when his phone buzzed.

Carefully, he closed the door then walked down the hall to his bedroom, half expecting to find a message from one of his teammates ribbing him for some reason or another. Instead, he found an email in his inbox.

One he hadn't been expecting.

Max,
I hope your dog is doing better. Sorry you and Brayden (and pooch) are going through that. Pets are sometimes more family than our actual family.

Thank you for letting me know about Mandy. I'm going to reach out to her.

Sincerely,
Angelica Shallows

He frowned at the strangely formal email, reread it a half-dozen times then spent way too long crafting a response.

Angel,
Sparky (I'm not to blame for the pup's terrible name) is
doing much better. It turns out he has IBS, which is treat-
able with very expensive food and daily medication.
However, I consider the expense worth it because Sparky is,
as you said, now part of our family. Plus, he makes Brayden
smile and I'd do almost anything to see my son smile. He's
been through too much upheaval in his young life.

I do hope you'll reach out to Mandy. She would very
much like to get to know her sister. Especially now.

-Max
P.S. Your cat is adorable and now Brayden wants one. I
blame you. :)
P.P.S. I suck at emails so feel free to text me any time
415-555-1234

Max pressed send and then held his breath for several long moments, wanting an immediate response, wanting her to email back, to text him right then. He knew it was ridiculous. She was a busy woman and had her own life. Plus, she'd already taken time out to check up on Sparky; that was progress and showed . . . what?

That she was a nice person?

He knew that already. She hadn't wanted to ruin Mandy's moment months before, had left instead of creating a scene.

If she'd been anything like Suzanne, Angie would have made a scene.

Stolen the moment for herself, diverted all focus to her.

Angelica *hadn't* done that. She'd left Mandy to her celebration.

Which also meant she was running scared.

After the talking to her at the vet's, he understood her actions better. She'd been hurt, violated, assaulted. She'd had baggage *for days*—baggage that wasn't her fault, but baggage that still complicated everything anyway.

Because he had Brayden. Because *he* had baggage of his own.

And his son had asked for a new mom.

Which couldn't happen for a multitude of reasons: Suzanne, Max's career, a need to protect his son from a parade of women. He'd promised himself he wouldn't do that. It would be just Brayden and him until his son was older.

They had Anna; they had a good life.

That was enough.

So, why *didn't* it feel like enough?

His phone buzzed again, this time with a text from an unknown number.

Max's heart leaped, pulse pounding in the base of his throat. He opened the message.

I'm glad Sparky's okay. Also, Sparky is not such a bad name for a dog.

His lips curved.

It's a horrible name and terribly unfitting given today's events. He should be called Puke-Monster or Barfy.

He searched for and sent a GIF of a gagging little girl before he realized that Angie might not be into that particular brand of humor.

"Shit," he muttered, toeing off his shoes and flopping back onto his mattress.

Max really sucked at this flirting thing.

Talk of puking and juvenile GIFs? Ridiculous. Except . . . he was realizing that he was at the point in his life where he was comfortable in his own skin. He *was* juvenile sometimes, silly GIFs made him laugh, and he found that he didn't want to apologize for being who he was any longer. *Finally*, he was comfortable in his own skin, so screw anyone who decided that wasn't good enough.

Even if she was an amber-haired beauty with a body that made his dick feel like it was alive for the first time in several years.

Max slipped off his pants and tossed his shirt aside, all while waiting for his phone to buzz with a response and yet pretending not to.

"Slick," he said, pushing up from the bed and heading to the bathroom to brush and floss his teeth. "Super, super slick, Max." He was still holding his cell, still half-hoping for a response that wasn't coming. "Whatever," he finally grumbled and set his phone on the charger.

Then saw there were two unread texts on his screen.

"Idiot." It was after midnight, so his phone was on Do Not Disturb.

Fingers fumbling, he opened the messages.

Talk about terrible names! Barfy is just mean. I like to think that Sparky is short for Spartacus and I think you should too.

Two minutes later, she'd sent another message, this one rivaling the formality of her earlier email.

I'm sorry if I woke you. I know you must be tired after your game this evening. I'll let you head off to bed.

Shit. He sank back onto the bed. Is this what dating was like nowadays? Technology dominating and sometimes hindering—the Do Not Disturb function on his cell all but cockblocking him? This was pathetic. It was so . . . he didn't know. Just not what he wanted.

Well, you want a woman you've nicknamed Angel and that alone speaks to a problem inside your brain, you fucking numbskull.

And *that* particular thought wasn't helpful now, was it?

Ignoring it, he sent another message.

You still up?

Thirty seconds passed before he saw her begin to type out a reply.

Yes.

Max called her before he could talk himself out of it. Just ignored the pounding of his heart, the way his palms went sweaty like a teenaged boy and hit the call button.

The phone rang and rang.

And rang.

TWELVE

Angie

SHE'D SPENT the last fifteen minutes pacing a circle in her apartment. First, the email.

Then she'd texted him!

For once in her life, she felt like she had big ol' lady balls.

Giant ones.

Brass ones.

Buzz. Buzz.

Angie glanced down at her hand, at the cell resting on her palm. "He's calling me," she whispered.

Buzz. Buzz.

"Oh, fuck nuggets." He was *calling* her. Oh God. What was she going to say? She couldn't answer it. Except, he'd just asked if she was up.

Buzz. Buzz.

She was going to pretend that she'd fallen asleep. That was all she could do.

"Yeah, you fell asleep in all of five seconds, you nitwit?" she muttered. Fuck. She *had* to pick up. She had to.

Okay, no biggie. This was just like email or texting, except with actual vocalizations. Totally doable. She swiped a finger across the screen. No problem at all. This was—

She dropped the phone.

"*Fuck*," she muttered, dropping to her knees and hurrying to scoop it up. "Shit. Fucking fumbling fucking fingers." She put her cell up to her ear. "Hel-hello?"

"You've got a dirty mouth."

All of her breath left her. Just whooshed right out of her lungs, her mouth.

Heat flooded into its place.

"Angel?"

She struggled to regain her ability to speak. "Yes."

Not exactly an articulate statement, but it was a word and one that fit the circumstance.

"You okay?"

"Uh-huh," she squeaked before sucking in another breath.

"I wasn't criticizing you," he said softly. "It's sexy hearing a woman who can use the many forms of the word *fuck*."

She snorted, and suddenly her lungs were working again. "Why do I feel like that's a line?"

"It's not."

His voice was like liquid honey, running over her nape, dripping with sticky sweetness down her spine.

"Why did you call me, Max?" she asked, and if *her* voice was slightly breathless, then so what? She wasn't going to tell anyone.

"I wanted to hear your voice."

"Now *that* definitely is a line." She could sense his smile. "You're grinning. I know it, so I'm right," she said, triumphantly.

"Maybe I am, but you'll never know."

If they FaceTimed, she'd know. But, Angie glanced down at herself, taking in the hole-filled sweats, the wine-stained T-shirt.

Yes, she said wine-stained, because even though she'd sent the email—*and* the text—it had taken half a bottle of red wine for her to work up the courage.

"I can hear your smile through the airwaves," she said. "Your voice changes."

"Like a boy going through puberty?" he asked.

Now he was frowning.

"No." Angie held her cell between her ear and shoulder as she gathered up her bottle and wine glass. She needed to keep moving, to not focus on the fact that she was talking to Max.

Max.

"Then what?"

She sank into the armchair in her room, covering her lap with a blanket. The bed was tempting her, its cozy white duvet and flannel sheets would be much appreciated on the cold evening, but it felt too . . . intimate to be lying there, chatting with Max when he made all the nerves in her body feel as though they were on fire with just a simple conversation.

"Angel?" he prompted, making her realize that she'd been quiet for too long.

"It gets warmer," she blurted. "I noticed when you talked with Brayden. Your lips tip up at the edges."

"Hmm," he said.

"I'm not crazy," she snapped.

Now Max's voice was genuinely concerned. "I didn't say you were, sweetheart."

"Oh."

"Yeah," he murmured. "*Oh.*" Not snarky or condescending, just a quiet *oh.*

Angie sighed and let her head flop back onto the chair. "I suck at people."

"That's not true."

"It *is*," she moaned. "I was an only child growing up, I was homeschooled, and I'm an engineer. Not that there's anything wrong with any of those, just that with my parents and my upbringing and my weird awkward personality—" She broke off with a groan

"You suck at people?"

"Exactly." Huffing, she pushed to her feet and crossed over to her bed, tugging the covers over herself.

If she was going to be like this—read, strange—then she might as well be comfortable.

"I don't think you suck. I think you're nice and sweet and beautiful."

Angie froze.

"And that's not a line."

Her laugh was a little brittle, but it softened, rounding at the edges as Max joined in with her.

"There you are."

"Yes," she whispered.

"Great," he said. "So, now you can tell me what your favorite movie is."

"*Empire Strikes Back.*" Not one iota of hesitation; she loved that movie so much.

"Are you serious right now?"

"Um, yes?"

"Because that's *my* favorite movie."

Angie felt his grin, and her heart skipped a beat, but somehow, she was able to . . . what? Shore up her courage? Feel comfortable enough to be herself? To crack a joke? Whatever it was, she *was* relaxed enough to say, "No way. It's mine. You can't have it."

In all her life, she'd never really teased anyone.

She hadn't had that type of relationship with her mom and she certainly hadn't been secure enough in herself to tease her father.

Work held a certain distance she'd always found comforting and safe. The people there were either her employees or her boss, so she needed to preserve a certain amount of professionalism.

But Max was different.

She thought that maybe things could be different with him.

"Pish," he told her. "I'm older. I saw it first, and thus, I own it."

"No way," she said. "I've seen it at least several hundred times. I can quote every line, even the Wookie sounds."

Wookie sounds?

Angie mentally groaned.

Was she fucking serious? She wasn't supposed to admit to a man she liked that could make mean Wookie sounds. That sounded insane.

"*Arrr!*"

She blinked. "Uh—"

"*Arrgh. Who. Arghhg.*" A pause. "In Wookie language that means, 'It is *mine.*'"

"You're lying."

He cracked up. "I am. Brayden thinks it's funny when I do that, because it's pretty much the only impression I can do."

"Pretty much?"

A chuckle. "Fine. The *only* impression I can do."

"That's still pretty"—she yawned—"good," she said.

"You're tired."

"I have to get up early for work in the morning."

"I'll let you go," he said gently.

"No." Another yawn. She was pleasantly buzzed, snuggled beneath her blankets and being serenaded by a gorgeous male voice. It wasn't exactly a surprise that sleep was drawing her in. Yet, she didn't want the conversation to end.

"Angel—" he began.

"Tell me about the game," she said.

"It was a shitshow. Sometimes it's like that—no bounces, can't quite slide into that groove."

"And Brit wasn't playing," she murmured.

"You really do watch, don't you?"

"It's my sister's team," she told him, burrowing into her pillow and closing her eyes. "I couldn't *not* watch."

"Yeah."

"And then I met you, and . . ."

"And what?" he prompted.

Her breathing slowed, her words sounding almost slurred. "And I felt something. For the first time in an eternity, I felt something."

"Me too."

She smiled, her eyes slid closed.

"Goodnight, Angel," he murmured.

"'Night."

Angie slipped off into oblivion just as Max hung up.

THIRTEEN

Max

MAX HAD JUST DROPPED Brayden off at school—on time and with no panic, so gold star for him—when his phone rang. He pressed the button on his steering wheel to answer the call, eyes staying firmly glued on his surroundings.

A good ninety percent of the time he felt like the kids and their parents were playing Frogger, only the object of the game was for him to not run them over.

Parents barely stopping before opening their minivan door and shoving their kids out into the street. Students popping out from between cars, forcing him to slam on his brakes. Crossing guards jumping out into the crosswalk without looking.

It was the perfect definition of a shitshow.

"Hello?" he said, carefully navigating past the school.

"Max."

Suzanne.

His heart frosted over, but this was his son's mother and he was determined to keep things civil. "Hi," he said.

No, it wasn't puppy dogs and rainbows, but the greeting *had* been polite, okay?

Sort of.

"Max—" She broke off.

A kid darted out in front of his car, and he slammed on the brakes with a stifled curse. Fuck but school drop-off was bound to give him gray hairs.

"This isn't the best time, Suzanne," he said, careful again to keep his tone neutral. "What can I do for you?"

"I'm—" She sighed.

And he knew that sigh. It was the start of a long and complicated conversation, one that would no doubt have him pulling out all of those freshly grown gray hairs. He'd been with Suzanne since high school, knew how she operated. Delaying this talk would only make things worse.

The best thing was to buckle down and get through it.

"Hang on," he told her and cleared the next intersection before finding a spot to pull over. "Okay, I've parked. What's going on?"

"It's early for you to be driving," she said. "I thought you'd still be in bed."

"School starts at eight."

"Oh."

Yeah. *Oh.*

As in, Suzanne was the mother of a school-aged boy. Yes, she might have forgotten that fact, but Brayden still had her DNA.

"Brayden misses you," he said.

So much so that he wanted Max to find a woman to fill that void.

"I'm pregnant."

He blinked, fingers tightening on the steering wheel.

"Say something."

Fuck. *Fucking*. Mother. Fucker. *How could she?* He sucked in a breath, released it slowly. "Well, we're divorced, and you're a grown woman," he said. "You're allowed to do what you want."

A long hesitation.

"I want to come home."

Two years ago? The answer probably would have been yes. But now? He and Brayden had been through too much for him to bring his ex back into their home.

"That's not possible." Max knew his tone should be softer, that the mother of his child was clearly distraught. But where in the ever-loving fuck did she get off? She'd abandoned them, abandoned Brayden. She'd *hired* the woman who he'd supposedly knocked up.

Yeah. Seriously.

He'd been playing in L.A. at the time and the season had been a tough one, longer road trips than normal, a new coach who required extra practices and outside team-building exercises.

Brayden had been four going on five and had just missed the cutoff for kindergarten. He'd been hell on two legs, busy as fuck, and only in preschool for three hours a day. Max got it, knew that it was exhausting, that he was little help when he was out of the state, and Suzanne had always wanted to go to this fancy resort in Mexico.

He'd met with a travel agent and planned a week-long trip for her and her best girlfriend at the resort. He'd picked out and paid for spa packages—hair treatments, nail stuff, massages, the whole works—for them both.

And the last piece of that was a new wedding ring.

He'd been in the minor leagues when they'd gotten married, so her ring was smaller and less fancy than a lot of the WAGS—wives and girlfriends—on the team. Hell, it was tiny when compared to Los Angeles standards.

Suzanne had waxed poetic about a particular jewelry designer for years.

Half of her Pinterest board was devoted to the designs.

Max had set up a meeting with the young woman, Colette Sandindo. She was already visibly pregnant—this was important because Colette was the woman Suzanne had paid to say Max had knocked her up. It didn't matter she was already in that state when he'd first met her. However, *because* she was pregnant when he demanded a DNA test to clear his name, her attorneys filed a motion that the court approved, making him wait until the baby was born before it was completed.

Four months.

That was how long he'd had to wait.

Not long in the grand scheme of things, but a fucking eternity when your story goes viral and suddenly you're someone's supposed baby daddy.

The sad thing?

Colette had delivered on the ring.

It was sitting in a box at the back of his closet. Pathetic, huh? But he hadn't been able to bring himself to chuck it into the Bay. Not when some poor innocent creature might choke on it.

Max Montgomery. Pro hockey player. Adulterer. Killer of sea creatures.

Perfect.

He sighed. "You can't come home," he repeated. "I'm sorry, but I've worked too hard getting Brayden on a schedule."

"Fuck a schedule. I need—"

"Suzanne. You terminated your parental rights. You don't *need* anything." He plunked his head down onto the steering wheel. "I pay you alimony, and I am happy to keep my verbal promise of renting you an apartment nearby so that we can arrange for you to see Brayden on a regular basis. But you can't live with me again and especially not with—"

"I'm not a whore," she snapped. "These things happen, or maybe you don't remember."

What had happened to the woman he'd married?

Or maybe the question should be: how had things gotten to this point?

"Do you want me to start looking for a place nearby?" he asked instead of replying to her statement. Somehow, his typical anger when dealing with his ex had faded, morphed into . . . nothing.

No. That wasn't it.

He was tired. Drained. Not able to summon up outrage any longer.

Because Suzanne didn't really matter.

"I fucking hate San Francisco." Her tone was sharpened to a knife's edge. "You know that."

"Okay then," he told her. "Brayden's doing great. I'm doing great. Thanks so much for asking." Max reached a finger for the end button on the steering wheel as she sputtered. "Nice talking with you. Hope everything works out. Take care—"

"Max—"

"Bye, Suzanne."

He hung up, blew out a breath, and waited for her to call back.

She did, approximately a heartbeat later, but he rejected the call, turned on his Do Not Disturb while driving, and headed back to his house.

He needed to get a meal in, do his daily workout, and then he was supposed to be helping in Brayden's class.

Something about cutting out paper flowers.

"Poor teacher." He had the feeling his hands weren't going

to be the best for that particular task. He could just pretend the kids had done the cutting and not him, right?

Max chuckled and flicked on the radio.

"The Imperial March" flooded through the speakers—Brayden's recent addition to their shared playlist.

That reminded him of Angie and her love for *Star Wars*.

Somehow—despite Suzanne's news, despite the unpleasant phone call, despite the sharp right turn his life had taken *because* of his ex—he smiled.

Just *thinking* about Angie made him smile.

A woman who made him smile. Now wasn't that a change?

He drummed his fingers on the steering wheel and thought of another thing that made him smile: thinking of Angie's reaction when she saw what he'd sent to her office.

FOURTEEN

Angie

SHE STARED at the monstrosity on her desk and tried to figure out what in the hell was going on.

Okay, monstrosity was probably an unfair word, but scattered on top of her formerly neat and organized desk was confetti.

"What the—?"

The confetti almost distracted her from the bouquet of flowers.

Except they weren't flowers.

Yes, there were stalks and they were wrapped in cellophane and paper like a typical bouquet, but instead of flowers, they were sticks with cute little plushies propped on one end.

Star Wars plushies.

"Oh, my God," she said, finally realizing that the confetti was shaped like droids. "How—?" Angie shook her head, picked up the envelope, tore it open.

Then felt her heart skip a beat.

In fairness, she'd suspected who it was from, but until she saw his signature on the note, she hadn't really believed it.

Her eyes trailed back up the card before her brain finally processed what was written on it. Laughter bubbled in her chest.

Angel,
Argh grrargh arr arg Rrrrugh.
Translation: Have dinner with me Friday.
Max

"*What* is that?"

Kelsey came up to her desk. "Is that confetti?" She shuddered.

"Yes, that part is terrible. But *look.*" Angie held up the note.

Kelsey took it, a little furrow appearing between her brows. "What the fuck is this?" she asked, turning the paper around.

"It's Shyriiwook."

Kelsey blinked. "Was that English?"

"It's Wookie."

Another blink.

"*Star Wars,*" Angie said, exasperated. "You need to turn in your nerd card, dude. But I emailed Max last night and then we talked on the phone and . . ."

How could she possibly explain?

"You talked about *Star Wars?*" Kelsey asked.

Angie nodded. "That and other stuff. I don't know. It was silly, I guess, because part of me felt like I was in high school or something. I was so giddy and he . . . said I was beautiful."

"Sounds like he's got at least one thing going for him," Kels said.

"What's that?"

"His eyes work." Her lips twitched. "Gross use of confetti aside."

Angie snorted, started piling up the confetti. "Yeah, I don't know what he was thinking with that."

"Men need to be trained—"

Jordan, their boss's brother and the former owner of Robo-Tech, chose that moment to stride by. "I resent that statement. Though"—he smirked—"it *may* be true."

He waved and left them chuckling, striding down the hall to Heather's office.

"You going to go out with him on Friday?"

"I—" Angie's throat went tight, but it wasn't just with panic this time. No, it was with excitement. "I—yes. I think so."

"Think?"

Angie bit her lip. "Okay. Yes, I am."

"Yes!" Kelsey fist-pumped. "Look at us, grabbing the world by its balls." They both wrinkled their noses. "Bad analogy," Kels said. "But you get what I'm saying. So, Friday you have plans, but want to go to the hockey game with me on Thursday? My brother has a box at the Gold Mine."

Angie frowned. "Sebastian has a box?"

"No, my other brother," Kels said. "Devon."

"Your brother is *the* Devon Scott?" Angie gasped.

Kelsey rolled her eyes. "God, why does everyone say it like that?"

"Because he was a fucking great player, and he's hot. Wasn't he named the Sexiest Man in—"

Kels gagged. "Don't. I can't with that. So, game Thursday?"

Angie sucked in a breath. "Well, I'm not sure."

"Why? Is it the crowd that's too much? We can do something else."

"I—it's not that. Just that . . . you know Wookie Max?"

Kelsey's brows drew down and together. "Uh, yeah?"

"Well, he's kind of Gold Max, too."

Her jaw dropped open. "Holy— Max *Montgomery?* Seriously?"

Angie nodded. "Yeah."

"Hot damn, he's sexy. Those piercing blue eyes." Kels fanned herself. "I saw him once at a pool party at Devon's house. Dude, his *abs.*"

Angie sucked in a breath. "I can't speak for his abs—"

"Yet!" Kelsey interjected.

"Yet," Angie amended, and it was funny how that admission might have made her freak in the past—hell, even yesterday— but now it seemed fine. Okay, not *fine,* exactly, but terrifying and wonderful and exciting, and . . . she was game to see Max's abs.

That in of itself made her feel like cheering because *finally* she'd had a normal female reaction. But—

"Is it weird if I go to the game?" she asked. "I mean, I guess it feels slightly stalkerish to accept the date on Friday then like go . . . evaluate him or something on Thursday."

Not to mention the fact that it was also her sister's place of employment.

The sister she still hadn't emailed.

"No." Kelsey made a dismissive sound and sat down on the edge of Angie's desk, helping her gather up the confetti. "It's a few friends getting together. Hell, Sebastian might come along with Rachel, and then you can call it work."

"There's also another piece," Angie said.

Kelsey rubbed her hands together. "More dirt! Give it to me now."

"First off, you're ridiculous," Angie told her. "Though you *are* extremely helpful, even though I think it comes out of nosiness."

"Well, that's a given."

"Second," she said. "And this is the honest truth, I'm not sure I can tell you. It's family stuff, and it's . . . not only *my* story to tell."

Kels made a face. "Ugh. Fine, be all reasonable, why don't you?" She bumped her shoulder against Angie's. "I get it. I do. I mean I *am* nosy as hell and want to know every detail, but I can occasionally be a responsible adult and control myself."

Angie sighed, though her mouth was curving. "Sucks, doesn't it?"

"So much!" Kelsey groaned. "But I'll survive." She chucked a pile of confetti in the trash. "Here's what we'll do. I'll email you the ticket and you can figure out if you want to go or not. No pressure either way."

Impulsively, Angie reached out and hugged her. "Thanks."

"Any time." She squeezed her back before standing. "And when you want to dish . . ."

"You'll be the first one I call. Scout's Honor."

"Were you a Girl Scout?"

Angie snorted. "Yeah, that's a no. An anxious girl doesn't mix well with the nature and the outside world."

Kelsey raised her hand as though making a very important proclamation. "Well, I've decided that doesn't matter because I'm holding you to your promise. Kelsey Scott is the first stop for all Angie/Max/future undetermined-and-hereto-unnamed-Angie-related gossip." She pretended to bow. "I'm ever at your service."

Angie saved one of each type of the confetti, carefully putting them in the paperclip holder in her top desk drawer before sweeping the rest into her trash can.

"So magnanimous."

"You know it." Kels left with a wave, only to pause a few feet away. "Don't let the confetti distract you from texting yummy Max. I think he picked the right type of flowers, don't you?"

Angie glanced down at the little plushies—Chewy, Luke, Han, Rey, and Leia, they were all there.

"Yes," she said, after fluffing Chewy's fur. "You're definitely right."

Except, when she glanced up, Kels was already gone.

She was going to keep Angie on her toes, that was for sure. But, with a soft chuckle, she pulled out her phone and sent Max a message.

And for once, she didn't overthink it. Just typed out a reply and hit send.

Serious personal growth. It was happening.

FIFTEEN

Monday

ANGIE: Thank you for the *Star Wars* bouquet. It's freaking adorable.

Max: I'm glad you liked it.

Angie: That being said, if you send me confetti again, I will find a way to get you back.

Max: I like the sound of that. What would you do?

Angie: *squinty eyes* I'd start by paying off the refs in your game tonight.

Max: How would you do that?

Angie: I know people.

Max: Hopefully not important people because I may or may not have sent you a confetti super pack.

Angie: That better not actually be a thing.

Max: Oh, it's a thing.

Angie: I hope you'll enjoy spending the night in the penalty box.

Tuesday morning

Max: How much did you give them?

Angie: Give who what?

Max: The refs. Three penalties last night. WTF.

Angie: Don't doubt my superpowers.

Max: I've canceled the confetti.

Angie: Good.

Max: Brayden has a school event tonight, but can I call you tomorrow?

Angie: I'll think about it.

Max: Do I have to break out my Wookie again?

Angie: *God,* no. I have a late meeting, but I'll be home by seven.

Max: Brayden's usually in bed by eight-thirty, okay if I call you then?

Angie: No more confetti EVER.

Max: Deal.

Angie: Then eight thirty works for me.

Max: Talk to you then.

SIXTEEN

Max

IT WAS MIDWAY through the third period when Max happened to glance up and see Devon Scott on the jumbotron. Devon was with his wife and others in his box. Max's gaze started to slide back to the ice when he saw—

Holy shit. Was that Angie?

Fuck. It *was*.

She was grinning and waving at the camera, a blonde that he thought was Devon's sister at her side and doing the same.

His eyes drank her in, desperate for any glance of her.

They'd managed to text for a few minutes every night and then had actually talked for a few hours last night, expanding on their favorite movies and TV shows, talking about comics and Marvel characters, what it was like to be a single dad, the projects Angie was working on at RoboTech. Unfortunately, it had been a crazy week for both of them at work, and Max hadn't found time to pop in to her work with a special delivery of confetti—*cough* real flowers this time—as he'd planned. Which meant he was ramped almost to fever pitch, he was so looking forward to their date tomorrow.

Max had it all planned out.

Anna was taking Brayden to see a movie and then they were having a sleepover at her house.

Not that he was expecting anything—though frankly, he wasn't opposed—but he just didn't want to put any limits on where their date would go.

Or risk Brayden and Angie crossing paths.

The last thing he wanted to do was trigger his son's ideas about getting a new mom. *That* wasn't happening.

As far as he was concerned, love was the dirtiest four-letter word around.

Except, if he truly believed that, then why initiate the date?

Angie wasn't a one-night stand. She was worth so much more.

Blane jabbed an elbow into his ribs. "What the fuck are you looking at?"

Max blinked, saw the screen was showing his team lined up and ready for the face-off. "Nothing," he muttered, knowing he needed to concentrate on the last ten minutes of the game, not whether or not he could catch Angie before she left.

Because he *really* wanted to catch her before she left.

The whistle blew, the puck dropped, and Max forced his brain to focus back on hockey.

But it was painful . . . his mind had drifted to the upper bowl.

———

HE GRABBED his cell the moment he reasonably could—after their coach, Bernard, had spoken to them and after Stefan had given the celebratory puck to the player he'd thought was the best of the game.

Blue, that night. He'd not only put them off to an early lead, he'd also gotten a hat trick—three goals in one game.

So, it was well-deserved.

Even though Max wished the festivities had taken less time.

Regardless, he dialed Angie's number on his cell, slipped out into the hall, and hoped she would pick up.

She did. With a rush of noise and a harried, "He-llo?"

"Don't leave yet," he said.

"What?"

"Don't leave," he repeated.

"Hang on," she said, and the noise muffled. He could barely make out her say, "Go on, I'll see you tomorrow at work." Then she was back on the line. "Max?" she asked.

"I'm here."

"Dang. Sorry, it's so loud I can barely make out what you're saying. Hold tight." The din of voices in the background slowly faded. "There," she eventually said. "I managed to find a quiet corner. Are you okay? Is Brayden all right?"

The fact she asked after his son undid him.

She'd met Brayden *one* time.

"Brayden's fine," he said.

Her relieved breath slid right into his exposed heart, curled deep inside. "Good. But now's not really a good time. I'm kind of tired and—"

"Don't leave." Repeated sentiment, but hopefully one she heard this time. "Don't leave without letting me see you, at least for a few minutes."

Her laughter was nervous. "Leave where?"

"Angel, I saw you on the jumbotron."

"Oh." Air rustled through his speaker. "It's not what you

think. My friend from work invited me. I wasn't trying to check up on you or—"

"I *like* that you came," he said. "I liked seeing you up there."

Her breath caught, her only response another, "*Oh.*"

"Come down?" he asked.

"I—uh—I can't."

"You don't want to see me?"

She coughed. "I—that's not it. I mean, I *want* to see you, it's just Mandy. She'll be busy, and if I run into her, I'll mess things up."

"That's not true," he told her then softened his tone. "You've made it this far. Don't you want to talk to her? To me? I can show you around, and maybe you'll be able to get rid of some of those regrets that are weighing you down."

Silence.

His gut twisted.

He'd blown it. Pushed too hard. It was one thing for her to see him, another to see Mandy. He didn't have the full story yet; he knew that. And still he'd pushed.

Max opened his mouth to apologize.

"I wonder if I'd do anything at all if I hadn't met Kelsey, or *you*, for that matter." Her tone was soft, almost questioning, and he sensed her shake her head. "I don't know why I let myself get peer pressured into these situations." Humor crept into her voice. "But let's hope this round yields as good of results as the first time."

He leaned back against the wall. "What kind of results did round one produce?"

"You."

A grin split his lips. "Oh."

"Yeah," she muttered and took a page out of his book. "*Oh.* Now, tell me how to get down there before I lose my nerve."

He felt like whooping but managed to play it cool. Just

barely. "Head to the elevators outside section 101, and I'll have someone come up and meet you. I just need to shower, and I'll be ready to go."

"O-okay."

His heart clenched at the wobble in her voice. "Stay strong for ten more minutes, okay?"

"Okay," she said, a little stronger.

"That's my girl."

Her breath caught.

"I'll see you in ten."

He hung up and hurried back into the locker room, stripping down at record speed, all while shooting a text to Sara, Mike's wife.

Yes, that was a surefire way to start the Gold's gossip train, but he also knew Sara was really good at putting people at ease. *And* she was tough enough to not let Angie turn tail and run.

Max took the world's shortest shower then sprinted to the Family Suite.

He opened the door, saw the scene inside, and knew it was a good thing he'd sprinted.

SEVENTEEN

Angie

SHE'D DECIDED she was going to kill Max.

She was going to confetti his house, his car, his front yard. Hell, she was ready to move past confetti and straight to tearing off one of the toy-sized hockey sticks mounted to the wall of the Family Suite so she could shove it straight up his—

"Why is your face so wrinkly?"

Angie froze, glanced down at the adorable little girl with tight brown curls.

"Mirabel," an older woman with gorgeous coffee-colored skin and an embarrassed expression scolded. She was slightly familiar looking and beautiful. Not normal person beautiful, but striking, even by Hollywood standards. "We don't comment on the way people look," she added. "It's what's on the inside that matters—"

"Easy for her to say," Sara deadpanned. "Monique here is a former supermodel."

Ah.

That was why Angie's mind had pinged with recognition.

The pieces fell into place as she realized this was *the* Monique, who had been the face of several big name brands for many years and a renowned runway model. Angie just hadn't realized she'd married a Gold player.

Monique rolled her eyes. "I swear, Sara. You're the worst."

"You love me." Sara—who'd met Angie at the elevators and showed her to this room of hell, aka the Family Suite—touched Angie's shoulder. "This is Angie. She's with Max."

A half-dozen raised eyebrows turned in Angie's direction.

She raised her palms. "I'm not. I mean, I *know* Max. It just—"

Oh hell.

They were back to staring at her with those appraising expressions, as though their cold, dead eyes were trying to stare into her very soul.

Okay, so that was a lie. The ladies had been very friendly. It was just . . .

Social situations.

Yup. Those.

She was so awkward. What could she possibly have to talk about with these women? Monique was a former supermodel, Sara a former gold medalist, not to mention there was also a CEO and several gorgeous stay-at-home moms in the mix.

She was just Angie.

A mid-level manager who was the secret love child of a former hockey player and a Class-A asshole.

Oh, and Mandy's long-lost sister, there was that, too.

And considering she sucked in normal social interactions, adding all that baggage into *this* situation meant she was seriously considering turning Max into a man-sized popsicle.

Topped with confetti.

She sighed, met Sara's inquisitive gaze, and said, "Max and I met a few months ago."

Simple. To the point. That would feed the wolves.

Except . . . not so much.

"He's been holding out on us for *months*?" Monique asked with a gasp.

"How dare he!" Sara added.

"That's not what—"

Sara slid her arm through Angie's, started leading her to a room that was filled with black leather couches and numerous television screens.

She coaxed—*cough*, pushed—Angie down into one. "Tell me everything."

"—I meant," Angie finished.

The door to the suite opened, and now everyone's eyes shot toward it. Max strode into the room, smile dimming slightly as he took in the scene.

Angie popped to her feet, hurried over to him. She was awkward and annoyed and . . . scarily happy to see him.

As in, her heart had done a little jumping jack the moment he'd appeared.

"Max," Monique said. "Angie said you've been dating for months. How dare you not tell us?"

"Didn't Spence retire?"

Monique narrowed her eyes. "Yes."

"So, why are you here pestering my girl?"

"*Your* girl?" Sara asked with raised eyebrows. "I need details. Now."

Angie's pulse sped up at Max's words, but Monique's reaction was more apparent. She clapped her hands together. "You've got a *girl!* Oh my God! I'm so happy for you."

"She makes weird wrinkly faces," Mirabel said, mirroring her mom's excited stance. "I want her to show me how to do that."

Angie snorted.

She couldn't help it. This was just so bizarre.

And yet, somehow, it was comfortable?

Wow. She needed to put that particular thought aside to ponder later.

Max took her hand. "And *that's* our cue to leave."

He tugged her out into the hall, despite the protests they left in their wake, leading her down around the corner, pushing open another door, and only stopping once they were safely ensconced inside what looked to be an empty conference room.

Then he brought their clasped hands to his mouth and pressed a kiss to the back of hers. "Hi," he murmured.

She melted. "Hi."

"You okay?"

He nodded, his thumb making small circles on the inside of her wrist, her body drifting toward his. "I'm sorry they cornered you."

Angie blinked, remembered herself, and pulled her hand free. "You abandoned me to the wolves!" she accused, plunked her palms onto her hips. "You were all sweet and charming on the phone, and then you just threw me into the snake pit."

Max's expression dimmed. "The wives and girlfriends are actually really nice, once you get to know them."

Angie paced away. "Of course, they are," she said. "They were wonderful. Snake pit isn't fair, I just . . . God, I'm *so* damn weird. I couldn't even think of anything to say." She lifted one hand, pressed it to her forehead. "And apparently, I make wrinkly faces. Fuck. What does that even mean?"

Max made a noise, and she whipped back around to see he was holding back laughter.

"Oh my God. You're not seriously laughing. I made the worst impression."

"You"—he giggled, the jerk *actually* giggled—"didn't."

Angie tried to hold on to her frustration.

She failed.

Because then she was laughing, too, bending at the waist and laughing so hard tears streamed down her cheeks. "Wrinkly . . . face . . ." she gasped out.

"Show her . . ." Max was almost hysterical.

Then he wasn't.

Angie glanced up, held her breath as he closed the distance between them and reached up a hand. "Still okay if I touch you?" he asked, voice husky enough that all traces of humor left her.

It was all she could do to nod.

Max was . . . well, no man had ever asked to touch her before, and somehow that simple courtesy made it okay. There was also the fact that he was the first man since the attack to make her feel something. To lust and want and need.

She hadn't felt that since the assault.

Okay, if she were being completely truthful, she hadn't *ever* felt this draw to *any* man.

And then there were the texts, the calls, and conversations.

But it wasn't just her body. Her *heart* felt as though she knew him.

Max's thumbs were gentle as he swept away the tears from her cheeks. "So fucking beautiful," he murmured. "I couldn't look away when I saw you on that screen tonight."

She started to shake her head. Beautiful wasn't an adjective she could process.

She was just her, just normal, weird Angie.

His palms cupped her cheeks, stopped the shake mid-movement. His eyes locked onto hers. "Beautiful," he said, more firmly this time.

Her lips parted.

In an attempt to form a protest? To plead for his mouth to slant across hers?

Yes. The second one.

Instead, Max just stared at her. As though he were memorizing her face or gazing past her eyes to see the depths of her soul.

Her tongue flicked out, wet the corners of her mouth.

His expression went hot.

But still, his lips stayed several inches from hers.

He tucked a strand of her hair behind her ear, the rough pads of his fingertips making her shiver. His breath was hot on her cheek. It smelled like cinnamon, and she *fucking* loved cinnamon.

"Max," she murmured.

"Hmm?" he asked, fingers trailing down her throat, across her collarbone.

She shifted, thighs squeezing, the space in between them growing damp.

And Angie couldn't hold back the words, her plea. Even though they were out of her comfort zone, even though she'd never said them to another man before.

Max made her *feel* things she'd never experienced before.

He pushed her, tore away those barriers separating her from the rest of the world.

From him.

So, she took one more leap that evening and said, "Kiss me."

His mouth was on hers an instant later.

EIGHTEEN

Max

SHE TASTED like heaven and hell all mixed together.

Angie sighed the moment his lips touched hers, her body stiffening for a heartbeat before she melted against him, breasts soft against his chest, hips coming to rest against his.

He groaned, sliding his fingers from her cheeks into her hair, pulling her closer.

Her tongue tangled with his, her pelvis pressed against his erection, making stars flash behind his eyes.

It was incredible. It was *everything*.

But Max wanted more.

He wanted to strip her naked and fuck her right there on the conference table, to drop to his knees, spread her thighs wide and make her come with his tongue, and then he wanted to thrust home and push them both over the edge.

Which was exactly why he pulled away.

Angie wavered, and he caught her against his chest, both of them breathing hard.

"That was—" She shivered.

"Good?" he asked, not too steady himself. His head was spinning, his cock rock-hard. He'd never experienced a kiss like that. One touch of Angie's mouth and his blood had threatened to evaporate from beneath his skin, his brain . . . hell, *that* body part was still struggling to make sense of it all.

"Incredible," she said, nuzzling into his chest, the word almost drunk with pleasure.

He knew the feeling. Incredible didn't even begin to cover it, let alone encapsulate how natural it felt to wrap his arms around her, to hold her close and stroke a hand down her spine.

"You're a bad influence," he teased, mouth curving when she shot him a glare.

"*You* kissed *me*," she said, stepping back and putting her hands on her hips again.

Yeah, he really liked it when she did that, could seriously appreciate how the movement accentuated those perfect handfuls of breasts. Not to mention that when Angie was mad at him, when her pretty brown eyes were shooting fire, she forgot to be in her head so much.

He'd take a present, pissed off Angie, over a scared, distant one any day.

Beautiful—inside and out—in both versions, but only one of those had asked him to kiss her.

"Should I remind you that you asked me to?"

Her jaw dropped open, and Max couldn't help it. He kissed her again, sweeping his tongue in between those parted lips, loving the way she threw her arms around his neck and kissed him back.

"You're terrible," she said, a few minutes later, chest heaving, eyes still filled with fire.

"Well, *you're* amazing," he told her and tapped a finger to her nose.

She stepped back, crossed her arms.

"What?" he asked when she didn't say anything.

"I'm looking for your flaws," she grumbled. "You're perfect and hot and can kiss like a fucking god." A pause. "And I'm just me . . . the nerd who has a wardrobe consisting of pun-filled T-shirts and *Star Wars* dresses—"

Yeah. No. He wasn't going to let her slip back into herself again, wasn't going to let her shortchange how special she was. Fuck, he'd known her for such a short time and he could see that Angie was different.

Not in a weird way either.

Yes, she liked *Star Wars* and knew Wookie speak, but fuck it all, so did he. And he loved that she enjoyed the things he did. Nerdiness was equal to sexiness in his book.

For God's sake, Max was the biggest nerd of them all.

He played video games on the plane trips. *He* watched every SciFi or Fantasy movie he could get his hands on. *He* looked forward to sharing all of that nerd-dom with Brayden.

But nerdiness aside, what mattered more to Max was Angie's heart.

It was, all jokes aside, solid gold.

"Are we going to play Who's the Bigger Nerd?" he asked. "Because I think I'll win."

She snorted.

"No?" He tipped her chin up. "Good, I'm glad you acknowledge my greater nerdiness."

"Hey—"

Max kissed her again.

And, yup, sparks. Heat shot down his spine, arrowing straight for his cock. Yes, it had been too long since he'd been with a woman, but he'd never gotten this hard from a simple kiss. Chubbies were a given, raging boners, not so much.

Then there was the other feeling.

The potentially scary one.

Because it had the power to devastate him.

So, he kept it light.

He grabbed Angie's hand and closed her fingers over his erection. "You do it for me, m'kay?" Her hand twitched, and he groaned, hips thrusting forward before he managed to regain control and tugged her fingers off.

Her shoulders relaxed. "That's not a pity boner?"

He snorted. "Not so much."

She grinned. "Damn, and here I was working up a full head of anxious steam."

"Nice try." Max cupped her cheek. "Should I add to that steam? Or should we stay here and risk getting caught making out like a teenage couple?"

Angie's eyes were filled with a mixture of hope and fear. "You mean Mandy?"

He nodded. "She'll leave pretty soon."

Angie sucked in a breath and lifted her chin. "As much as I want to keep kissing you, I think I'm finally ready to do this."

"I think you are, too." He laced his fingers through hers. Such a short time and yet . . .

He knew her.

Angie was special.

And she already meant too much.

NINETEEN

Angie

HER HEART POUNDED LIKE A DRUM, and Angie would be lying if she'd said she wasn't nervous.

What the hell am I doing? Was pretty much playing on repeat in her brain.

And yet . . .

Her feet were still moving.

Max had taken her to an elevator and through several twists and turns before she was finally in familiar territory. Or semi-familiar, since she'd only been underneath the arena once.

A visit aborted by her sister's engagement—and now the visit was prompted by Mandy's pregnancy.

Plus Max.

And Kelsey. Angie couldn't discount her friend either. Or herself for that matter.

Life was funny sometimes. She'd done the work, put her time in at therapy, pushed herself slowly and inexorably out of her comfort zone, and yet all of that progress was dwarfed by her growth over the last few weeks.

Max stopped them a couple of feet from the door to the therapy suite. "You sure?"

Angie swallowed hard.

She'd delayed long enough.

It was time.

"Should I knock?" she asked.

"No need."

A nod, a deep breath, and she turned the doorknob.

The room was empty except for a group chatting in one corner. Angie knew they were players not only because they were head and shoulders taller than her, but also because their shoulders were wide and their thighs like tree trunks.

Her gaze trailed around the room, searching for any sign of Mandy and finding none; her stomach twisted.

Damn.

Max nudged her forward. "Her office," he said, taking her hand and tugging her across the space. He deposited her in front of another closed door. "You can do this," he murmured.

"Why are you doing this?" she asked.

He frowned. "Am I pushing too much?"

Angie shook her head. "No," she said. "I just—why are you being so nice? Why do you care when we barely—"

"Know each other?"

She nibbled at the corner of her mouth. "Well, *yeah*. I mean why are you invested in me? In this?"

Max inhaled and exhaled slowly. "At first, it was for Mandy. She's my family and I didn't want her to be sad." A shrug. "But that's not all of the story. I mean, I'm attracted to you, obviously, and want to get to know you better. I also think that most people would empathize with you and want to help . . ." He trailed off.

"And?"

"And—" Another breath, this one shorter and more staccato. "I'm drawn to you, Angel. I could list all the reasons why, starting with that big heart of yours, with the way you talked so sweetly to my son, how you checked up on me and Sparky, but those are not even the whole story either." He cupped her cheek. "I've never believed in instant *anything*—and certainly not instant feelings—but somehow with you, Angel, I feel like I've known you my whole life."

She bit her lip. "Me, too. I can't explain it, other than you somehow get me."

"It's because we have nerdy things in common." His handsome mouth curved.

Angie placed her palm over his, laughed softly. "We're nuts, aren't we?"

He grinned. "Yeah, probably."

"And what about Brayden? I don't want to take away time from him."

"Brayden will be fine," he said. "We'll go slow and steady and see where things go, okay?"

She sucked in a bracing breath. "Okay." Her lips twitched. "But you still owe me a date tomorrow. This doesn't count."

He saluted. "Noted."

"All right," she said. "Here goes."

And she knocked on Mandy's office door.

There was a thump and a male curse, followed by a "Shh!" Eventually, the door cracked enough to reveal Mandy's fiancé, Blane, his shirt buttoned wrong.

Blane glanced at her, then Max, his brows pulling together. "Um, can I help you?"

"H-hi." She lifted her chin. "I'm Angie. I, uh, wanted to see if Mandy was available—"

The door wrenched open.

"Angelica? Oh my God!" Mandy gasped, one hand coming up to cup her mouth.

Angie nodded. "Hi, I'm sorry it took me so long to—"

Mandy's eyes filled with tears. "Don't apologize and don't freak out. I'm going to cry because I'm a hormonal mess and I'm so happy to meet you finally. God, you're so pretty." She sniffed. "Can I hug you?" Her face screwed up. "I'm sorry, I'm so weird right now. Of course, I can't hug you. We just met. I—"

Angie wrapped her arms around her sister, squeezing tight. She was surprised to find that Mandy was several inches shorter than her, considering Angie always felt so small when compared to her.

After a few seconds, Mandy pulled back and took Angie's face between her palms. "You're so beautiful." Another sniff. "And you have Dad's eyes."

Angie blinked back tears herself. "So do you."

Mandy nodded. "I'm sorry I didn't know about you sooner."

"I shouldn't have stayed away for so long. I—uh—"

"There's probably a lot we both need to talk about," Mandy said. "Are you—? Do you—?" She covered her face. "I'm sorry. Usually I'm better with the English language than this."

"Breathe, sweetheart," Blane said, wrapping an arm around Mandy's shoulders. He extended a hand to Angie. "I'm glad to meet you."

She nodded. "Me, too."

And silence. She had so many things to talk about with her sister, but it was late and they were at the arena and—

"Do you want to grab lunch sometime soon?" she asked. "Both of you," she added hurriedly when Mandy exchanged a look with Blane. "I'd like to—well, I've been alone for a long time. I'd like to get to know my family."

"Are you—?" Mandy sighed. "*Ugh.* I was trying to find a tactful way to ask if you have a safe place to stay."

Angie frowned. "Um, yes? I bought an apartment in the city a few years ago."

"Oh."

Mandy's disappointment was so glaring that Blane stage-whispered, "She's in mother-bird mode. She wants to gather all her chicks and bring them home."

Mandy smacked him the same time as Max snorted.

Angie glanced back at him.

"Mandy's very good at organizing people," he agreed.

"That's not fair—" Mandy sighed. "Okay, *fine*. It is."

Angie straightened her ponytail nervously. "I'm, uh, all right. I've lived on my own for a long time and have a good job." Mandy's face fell, and Angie hurried to say, "I appreciate the offer though."

Mandy beamed and they spent a few minutes talking about Angie's job at RoboTech. They were just starting to tour the freshly remodeled therapy suite when Mandy let out a huge yawn.

"You're tired," Blane said. "We should—" He shut up when Mandy leveled a glare at him.

"Blane is right," Angie said, half to save him and half because it *was* late.

"I'm—"

"And I have to work tomorrow."

Mandy's face fell. "Oh gosh! I'm—"

"Give me your phone." The demand seemed to shock Mandy out of the apology and her sister didn't say anything further, just mutely reached into her pocket and pulled out her cell.

Angie input her number then sent herself a text.

"There," she said, handing it back. "Now we can figure out a good time to meet up again."

Mandy clutched it to her chest. "You're not going to d-disappear again, are you?"

That glimpse of emotion made Angie's heart skip a beat, her eyes burn with tears.

She *wasn't* going to vanish.

She was so beyond done with running.

But instead of admitting either of those things and risking starting some sisterly waterworks, Angie smiled and said, "And miss out on my chance to be the annoying younger sister?"

The waterworks came anyway. Mandy burst into tears and hugged Angie tight. "You're so funny!"

"Then why are you crying?" she asked.

"I don't know."

Angie sniffed.

"Why are *you* crying?"

Her lips twitched. "I don't know either."

After a long minute, they both pulled back. Mandy looked at her with her father's eyes. "I'm so glad to finally meet you."

Angie squeezed her sister one more time. "Me, too."

"God, we have so much to talk about!"

Blane slipped an arm around Mandy's shoulders again. "Soon, sweetheart."

She nodded. "I know." To Angie she said, "Run, before all of these questions I have in my head start bursting out of my mouth."

"Bye." Angie waved and turned for the door, Max trailing her. She'd just made it into the hallway when she heard Mandy exclaim, "Was she with *Max*?"

The man in question turned to her.

"Gossip train," she said.

He inclined his head. "More like gossip Ferrari, but the point is there."

She winced, trying to decipher how she felt about that, especially when things with Max were still new. It felt like they'd skipped a few steps. "Do you mind?"

He laced his fingers through hers. "Circle back to before. I like you, Angel," he said. "So, the more important question is, do *you* mind?"

Angie considered that as they navigated the twists and turns in the arena. It wasn't until they emerged out onto a parking lot that she'd ferreted out exactly what was going on in her mind. "No," she said. "I don't, even though the logical part of my brain is telling me that it's all too fast, and it's stupid to get wrapped up with a hockey player when my dad was . . . well, my dad. Not to mention Brayden and your ex and hell, my anxiety isn't something that I can pretend is just magically cured. It's work, and you may decide that you don't want that in your life." She squeezed his fingers. "Part of me feels like all of that together is a powder keg, destined to blow up and destroy us both."

"And the other part?" he asked carefully, leading her to a black SUV.

Her eyes met his. "The other part of me wants to grab on to this chance and enjoy it for however long it lasts."

Max released a relieved breath as he opened the car door and helped her inside.

"I like you, Max Montgomery."

He trailed his fingers along her jaw. "I like you, too, Angelica Shallows."

The gentle kiss he pressed to her lips stole a chunk of her heart.

TWENTY

Max

MAX STARTED to pull out of the player's lot then realized he hadn't even asked if Angie had her car there.

"Oh no," she said when he asked. "I took an Uber because I didn't want to deal with all of the crazy city traffic."

"I guess you're looking for a ride then?"

"You offering?"

"Only if you tell me where you live." He waggled his brows.

She rolled her eyes but that smile of hers, the one that never failed to make his own appear in return, crept out. "That's generally how these things work," she deadpanned before rattling off her address and directing him to her apartment.

"Have you seen the latest Marvel movie?" he asked.

"Uh, is that even a question?" she said. "Because the answer, of course, is absolutely. I've seen it three times already. It's..."

"Everything," he said. "Or at least, according to Brayden. He went with Anna opening weekend. It's been all I can do to avoid spoilers."

"Dude, that movie came out weeks ago. You're well out of the buffer period. Any spoilers you hear at this point are your own fault."

He stopped at a red light, turned to narrow his eyes at her. "I have a job that keeps me too busy to—"

"*I* have a job that keeps me busy," she teased. "Yours is just an excuse. You need to get on it, dude."

"No sympathy," Max grumbled.

"Nope," she said with a giggle. "Also, you're seriously making me doubt your priorities and your nerd degree. This is me." She pointed to a building.

"Let me find a spot to park, and I'll walk you up."

"No. It's late, and you should get home."

He braked, double-parking for the moment. Hell, this was San Francisco, double-parking was pretty much an art form. "Brayden is already asleep," he said. "I'm not in a rush, and the adrenaline from the game will keep me up for hours."

Angie yawned. "Well, it *was* an exciting game, and I'm glad you guys won, but I'm not going to be up for hours."

"It's late and dark."

She raised one brow, turned her head so she was looking out her window. "You can see inside my building from here. Plus, I have a doorman. I'll be fine."

He leaned close, nuzzled her jaw. "So independent."

"Damn r-right," she said, voice stuttering when he flicked his tongue out to taste her skin.

So fucking sweet.

"Or maybe you're trying to deny me my goodnight kiss?" Her lips parted in surprise, and he traced one finger along the bottom one. "No reply?" he asked, pressing a kiss to her cheek, the corner of that mouth. "Just gorgeous, sexy silence?"

Angie rotated to face him, the movement so fast he blinked in surprise. "So, that's how it is?" she said, lips a millimeter from his, her hot breath teasing and tempting all at once. "You only like me silent?" Her mouth brushed his.

Max stifled a groan when she leaned back, trailed one hand along the V of her blouse. The woman had gorgeous breasts, and he wanted to motorboat them like a son of a bitch. Especially when she caught him looking and arched her spine.

His mouth watered to taste.

"I like you, Angel," he said, his voice like sandpaper.

"Hmm," she said, unbuckling her seat belt so she was fully facing him, resting her elbow on the console and propping her jaw onto her palm. "I'm not so sure about that."

She licked her lips.

And he lost his mind.

One tug had her over the console and onto his lap. The next had her straddling his hips.

"Oh," she said and tilted her hips, brushing against his cock. "*Oh*. That's—"

He kissed her, taking advantage of her parted lips to slip his tongue inside. Fuck, but she tasted amazing. Fuck, but she *felt* amazing, soft to his hard, skin like silk, mouth hot and wet and—

She broke away.

Both of their chests were heaving, but fuck oxygen, fuck breathing. He needed Angie.

Naked and beneath him.

Or naked and on top of him.

His lips found hers again, and he groaned when Angie melted against him, breasts rubbing against his chest, pelvis shifting so she was seated more fully against him. She moved, and he groaned, stars flashing behind his eyes. Then she moved again and he came very close to embarrassing himself.

Yeah, not ideal.

He shored up every ounce of his control, lifted Angie from his lap, and deposited her back onto her seat.

"You're dangerous," he told her.

She clasped a hand to her throat. "*You're* dangerous."

He grinned.

She grinned.

Her words were soft, though her satisfaction was plain to see. "Thanks for the goodnight kiss."

"I—"

A horn blared behind them before a car swerved around them, the driver flipping them both off in the process.

"That's my cue," she said and reached for the handle.

He grinned. "Perfect timing, as always."

Angie laughed. "Thanks, Max. For everything." She hopped out.

"Wait," he said before she closed the door. "I'll still see you tomorrow?"

A smirk. "Only if you promise to take me to see the Marvel movie."

Marvel *and* a sexy woman? Yeah, not exactly a trial. But he played along anyway, tapping a finger to his chin as though pondering the statement. "Only if you promise me another goodnight kiss."

She bit back a smile. "You gonna spring for popcorn *and* candy?"

"I'll even throw in an ICEE if you want."

"Mmm, sugar," she teased. "Okay, I'm in."

She closed the door, and he watched her walk inside, smiling when she turned back to wave at him before she disappeared into the lobby.

Banter, superheroes, and scorching hot kisses?

This woman was *the one.*

TWENTY-ONE

Angie

SHE STUMBLED to her desk to find Kelsey perched on the edge, bright-eyed and bushy-tailed and totally ready to pounce.

"Hi," Angie said.

"Well, you look like the dead," Kels replied. "So, obviously you didn't get laid last night."

Angie plunked down in her chair and glugged some coffee. Then she stretched her arms above her head, resisting the urge to slap herself across her cheeks. "What nonsense are you talking about?"

Kelsey sighed, gripped Angie's upper arms, and shook. "You. Sexy time. Max. Many orgasms."

That snapped Angie out of her fatigue . . . at least for a moment.

She wasn't used to staying up so late on a work night and by the time she'd managed to calm herself down after the game, and Mandy, and then Max's kisses, it had been close to three in the morning.

And she usually got into the office at seven.

She shook her head. "You're crazy," she muttered.

"About the multiple orgasms?" Kelsey asked, way too innocently in Angie's opinion. "No way. He's got that look."

"*What* look?"

"The I'm-gonna-fuck-you-six-ways-to-Sunday look."

Angie blinked, really liking the image that particular statement brought to the forefront of her mind. Max naked and on top of her. Or her naked and Max beneath her or—

"He's so sexy."

"You've talked to him?" Angie asked, wondering why she was feeling the teeniest bit jealous when she had absolutely no right to.

No right. No claim. No sex.

Boo, said her vagina.

Probably smart, said her brain. *It's too soon.*

You want it anyway, said her vagina.

Of-fucking-course I do, said her brain.

So, go for it—

"Nope. But I've seen him at Devon's, remember? And on TV and in magazines and"—Kelsey fanned herself—"he's totally got the DILF thing going on. You need to sleep with him, find your happy place between the sheets."

Max *was* seriously hot and given the way their kisses had nearly melted her bones last night, she had to agree with Kels. They wouldn't have any problems with chemistry. But it wasn't just sex, or the anticipation of it, or the fact that she wanted him more than she'd ever wanted anyone else in her limited experience. He was sweet and funny and genuinely cared about the people he'd adopted into his family—whether that was by blood, like Brayden or by friendship, like Mandy.

"I'm really into him," Angie said. "It's going to be a serious problem."

Kels frowned. "Why?"

"Because I barely know him."

"So, *get* to know him."

Angie sighed. "That's just the thing. I'm normally so nervous to get to know people, all awkward and weird—case in point, drinks with your friends—"

"You know they're already *your* friends, too, right? We're like the mafia, once you're in, there's no getting out," Kelsey teased. "But seriously, I like you and they liked hanging out with you, too, so now you're stuck with us."

Angie's heart went warm and fuzzy. "I liked hanging out with them and you, too," she said, a self-deprecating smile twisting her lips. "*After* I spent the first half making it really fucking weird."

Kels snorted. "You weren't that bad," she said. "And I wasn't going to let that giant brain of yours get in the way of fun."

Angie rolled her eyes. "Your brain is bigger than mine."

"Is this how women do penis comparisons?" Kelsey tilted her head to the side, tapping a finger to her chin. "Your brain is bigger. No, *yours* is."

"Maybe." Angie chuckled. "Except for the fact that I don't think any man would willingly tell another man his penis was smaller."

Kelsey started giggling. "You're right."

"I've got ten inches, you're twelve," Angie said, deepening her voice and waving an arm in front of her pelvis. "You're bigger. You win, said no man ever."

"Twelve? Damn, girl." Kelsey's giggles continued, and this time Angie joined in.

"I have high standards," Angie joked.

That was it. They both started cackling, bending at the waist and not even attempting to pretend they were focused on something work-related. The elevator dinged while they were still in that state, and Jordan walked by her desk, pausing for a second before shaking his head. "Nope, I don't think I'm going to ask."

"Probably for the best," Kelsey told him.

He nodded and they watched him walk away, disappearing into Heather's office.

Angie turned to Kels. "Poor guy," she said.

"He'll survive," Kelsey replied then bumped her shoulder. "And that was a legit joke, girlfriend. A legit-non-awkward, dirty-minded joke. "When you forget about being in your head, you're . . ."

"Normal?"

Kelsey huffed. "Who says there's a normal? My point is that when you're not overthinking everything the world gets to see the real you." She bumped Angie's shoulder again. "And the real you is pretty damned great."

Angie felt her eyes burn. "Kelsey," she exclaimed. "That's not fair!"

"What? Emotions?"

"Yes. *Emotions.*" Angie sucked in a breath, released it slowly. "But seriously, thank you for pulling me out of my shell. I know I don't know you super well, yet, but I feel like we've been friends for a lot longer."

"You complete me." Kelsey drew a heart in the air. "So Max?"

Angie's heart fluttered. "He means something."

"I know. I can see it in your eyes," Kels told her. "They soften when you say his name."

"Damn. There goes my poker face."

Kelsey touched her arm. "I think you deserve someone who makes you feel that way, someone who makes you smile."

"You're sweet."

"I'm also extremely annoying."

Angie shrugged. "That's a given."

"Hey!" They both laughed again as Kelsey pushed up off the desk. "I guess we should get some actual work done, huh?"

"Probably."

"I don't *want* to," Kels whined.

"I know." Angie sighed. "And I didn't even tell you what happened between the end of the game and our make-out session in front of my apartment building."

"Oh, my God. He *kissed* you!"

"Dude. My tonsils are thoroughly checked."

"Was it as amazing as I've imagined?"

"What do you think?"

Kelsey grinned. "That I'm really fucking jealous right now."

"You should be."

Angie laughed at the outraged noise that came out of Kels' mouth. "Drinks tonight. Bobby's. You're going to tell me every last detail."

"I have a date with Max tonight."

"*Ugh.*" Kels shook a fist at the ceiling. "I'm so not good at delayed gratification. Fine. Saturday night. And I'm calling in the girls."

Angie smiled. "I'd like that."

"And you're going on the group chat."

"Heaven help me."

Kelsey snorted, turned to leave.

"Wait," Angie blurted. "What should I wear tonight?"

"Do you want it to just be a date?" She lifted her hands, as though weighing options. "Or do you want the fucking-you-six-ways-to-Sunday version?"

Angie bit her lip, heart pounding.

What *did* she want? To play it safe or to dive in headfirst and see where things laid? And that aside, she wasn't even sure she *could* sleep with someone this soon. What if she froze up? Plus, she wasn't the type of girl to—

No.

No more weighing all the pros and cons, worrying over every possible outcome.

This came down to something much simpler. This came down to how she felt in her gut, her heart.

Did she want Max?

Yes.

Did she trust him?

Her heart skipped a beat because . . . yes, she did.

And, for once in her life, she didn't want to let fear hold her back. She wanted to jump in feet first with a man who was nice and sexy and liked her for herself—nerdy, awkward, and occasionally a pain in the butt.

She wanted to shirk the anxiety that had held her back for so long and just *feel*.

She wanted to live.

And so, she turned to Kelsey, lifted her chin, and said, "I want the six-ways-to-Sunday option."

Kelsey's smile widened. "I know just the dress."

TWENTY-TWO

Max

HOLY FUCKING BREASTS, was the first thought that went through Max's head when he picked up Angie that evening.

She'd opened the door to her apartment, and his eyes had drifted from her gorgeous face straight down to her gorgeous—

Yes, he was a pig.

But *fuck* her breasts were amazing.

"I like your dress," he said, forcing the pig-like tendencies aside and returning his gaze back to Angie's. "You look beautiful."

She tucked her hair behind her ear. "It's not too much for the movies?"

"Fuck, no," he told her. "Especially because it means I get to try and sneak a look down your dress all night."

Her lips curved. "You already did that."

"And, believe me, I'm definitely not tired of *that* view." He bent slowly, giving her time to tell him to back off. That him moving close was too much too soon. Or maybe too presumptuous, despite what had happened in his car last night. But Angie didn't move. Instead, she rose on tiptoe, drifting toward him. He pressed a soft kiss to her lips. "Hi."

"Hi," she said, mouth brushing his again as she spoke.

"Hi." Nonsensical, but Max found that he didn't have the strength to step back. Not when she tasted so sweet, and he could smell the soft floral scent of her. Not when her skin felt like silk beneath his fingertips.

"Hi," she said, eyes sliding closed when their mouths brushed one more time. He cupped her cheek. "We're idiots."

"I don't think I care."

He kissed her again.

And not a soft, teasing brush of mouths. Instead, this time, Max made the contact count. He slipped both hands into Angie's hair and tugged her close, slanting his lips across hers and kissing her deeply.

Her tongue slipped into his mouth, making him groan with pleasure, and those glorious breasts pressed against his chest.

Fuck the movie.

He needed Angie naked and under him.

Alarm bells blared to life in his mind, and he started to pull away, to wrestle himself back under control. But when he slipped his hands from her hair, Angie grabbed the front of his shirt and yanked his mouth back down to hers.

Heat slid down his spine, tightening every muscle in his body, along with his cock.

Max let his tongue tangle with hers, allowed himself a few more moments of pleasure before he tugged Angie's hands free of his shirt and stepped back.

His chest heaved like he'd gotten stuck on the ice, desperate for a change.

But this wasn't anything like the torture of having to push through exhaustion, trying to suck in oxygen while his legs and lungs were burning, frantically trying to make a play so he could streak to the bench and get a break.

Instead, this was the best sort of exertion.

Of course, his was cock was hard enough to hammer nails, but he'd never felt more alive or exhilarated. Every nerve ending pulsed with need and awareness and *fuck*, he wanted her.

But he also knew he didn't want to fuck this up.

Which was all well and good until she released one hand from his shirt then reached down and grabbed his cock.

"Oh fuck," he groaned.

"Max?" she asked, stroking him through the cotton of his slacks.

He would be lying if he'd said his response was intelligible. The best he could say is that some sort of strangled sound emerged from between his lips.

"I have an idea," she said, releasing him to stroke her fingers up his chest.

He cleared his throat. "Yeah?"

She rose on tiptoe, stretching to whisper in his ear. "Yes."

"What's that?"

Her tongue flicked out. "Come inside, and maybe I'll show you." She turned and walked back into her apartment, hips swaying.

Max followed because while he might be a lot of things, an idiot wasn't one of them. Angie stopped a few feet inside the door, turning to face him, and *fuck* but he'd missed the fact that her dress was short and her legs were on full display.

And on her feet were fuck-me pumps with . . . droids on them.

His lips curved. "R2 is where I want to be."

"Uh"—her eyes flashed down to her shoes then back up —"what?"

He closed the door, striding over to her. Angie held her

ground, chin rising, but the nearer he got, the more quickly her breaths came, and the pinker her cheeks got. "I don't have a foot fetish," he murmured. "I want to be here." He brushed a finger over the dip in her dress, the lightest touch just between her breasts where the little blue and white droid sat.

"The . . . uh—" She sucked in a breath when he stroked the back of his knuckles there. "The whole dress is R2."

"I know." He nuzzled her neck. "I'm jealous of all of them."

Her hands came up and held him close when he kissed his way up and behind her left ear. "You like my"—a moan when he nipped the sensitive spot there—"my shoes too?"

Those heels.

Four-inch blue stilettos.

Hot as hell.

Her whole outfit was pure Angie—sweet and sexy with a little nerd thrown in and . . . it turned Max on like nothing else ever could. He loved that she was intrinsically herself. That she loved what she loved and didn't apologize for it.

He laced her fingers with his, allowed himself one more nuzzle of her neck before straightening. "I love them," he said. "But we should go if we're going to make our dinner reservations."

"About that," she began.

"Oh, yeah, I'm sorry," he said, squeezing her hand. "What did you want to show me?"

White teeth nibbled on pale pink lips.

Max's cock went even harder.

"Nothing. Well, that's not—it's something." She sighed, pushed back her hair with her free hand. "I'm so freaking awk—"

"Why did you ask me to come inside your apartment?"

Her cheeks flared red-hot. "Well, I mean, even though this is technically date one, I do feel like we've gotten to know each other pretty well over the last few weeks, what with us talking every night and the emails, then that day at the vet with Sparky." She shrugged. "That's not even including everything that happened last night . . ."

"Yeah?" he prompted when she trailed off.

"Ugh, I'm so bad at this."

Max had been following the conversation with anticipation, though that was quickly transmuting into fear. Had he pushed too much? Fuck, he knew Angie's backstory, he should have been more respectful, slowed everything way down.

"You're not," he told her. "You get to set the pace. You're in charge."

The blush dimmed. "Yeah?"

He nodded. "Yes. I mean it, too. I'm sorry if I moved too fast. This is all about you—"

Mischief crept into those pretty brown eyes. "Max?"

"Yeah."

"Want to know what I was really thinking when I invited you inside?"

"Of course, I do."

"I was thinking about how much I wanted you to come"—he frowned, wondering if nerves were making her repeat herself. Then he heard the rest of her words and they froze him in place, rocking him to the core—"inside of me."

Max blinked, stunned stupid.

Her blush picked up again. "I—uh—never mind. It's—"

What was that about not being an idiot before? Well, *stupid* was apparently a different story because it took him precious seconds to gather his wits and react.

He snagged Angie's wrist when she turned away and he stepped close, her back to his front. His cock ached, every cell in his body screamed at him to lift up her dress, drop to his knees, and make her scream out his name.

Instead, he traced gentle fingers down the bare skin of her arms, loving the way she shivered, how goose bumps prickled to life there. "Are you sure?" he asked softly.

She inhaled shakily, ass shifting and brushing his dick, making stars shoot behind his lids.

"Yes," she said. "I'm sure."

And so, Max did what he'd been dreaming about since the previous summer, the fantasy that had been swimming in his mind from the moment he'd seen Angie in her dress.

He spun her around and kissed her with every ounce of his desire.

TWENTY-THREE

Angie

GOOD.

That was the single thought she could muster.

Everything Max was doing just felt good.

He led her over to the couch, sat down and tugged her down into his lap, all while still kissing her. He kissed her until she ran out of breath, until she pulled back to gasp in oxygen, and even then, he *still* kissed her, only this time his mouth was on her cheek, her jaw, her throat.

She shivered when he traced his tongue across the tops of her collarbones, gooseflesh erupting all over her body.

"*Oh,*" she gasped when his tongue dipped into the low V of her dress.

He paused, brushed one finger across her cheekbone, and waited until she looked at him. "Hi," he said, lips curving.

Angie sucked in a breath, trying to settle herself when every nerve in her body seemed to be on fire. "Are we doing this again?"

He cracked a smile. "Maybe." He cupped her jaw. "You're so beautiful."

"I've never done this before," she blurted and watched as his face clouded, as he started to pull back. It was only then that she realized how he'd taken her words. "No," she said, cupping *his* jaw. "*Max.* I meant, I've had sex before"—with three people because she did not count the person who'd assaulted her in that number—"I just meant, I've never felt like this before. Never been this attracted, this attached so quickly. And I've never jumped into bed with a man this soon."

His expression darkened. "We don't have to do this," he said. "It doesn't *have* to be this soon. Let's go to the movie, to dinner. Let's spend some more time getting to know each other—"

She kissed him. "Don't you see? For the first in my life, I'm not scared and sitting on the sidelines. I *want* to leap." Her heart was pounding, but not from fear or anxiety. It raced because she wanted him.

"With you," she murmured, shifting so instead of sitting sideways on his lap, she was straddling him. "I want to take that leap with *you,* Max."

He swallowed hard. "You're sure?"

"You silly, sweet, *wonderful* man." Her smile was wide; she knew it was. But dammit, she just liked him so much. "I'm sure." A pause. "But know that you still owe me a date at some point."

His mouth quirked. "Deal," he said. "And it needs to include the movie. Frankly, it's a miracle that I've avoided spoilers this long anyway."

She was unreasonably happy.

Well, not unreasonably since she *was* with Max, but still giddy and excited and—he shifted underneath her, the hard length of his erection beneath his pants the best kind of tease.

"Deal?"

"I can get behind that." He raised a brow, and her cheeks went pink as she processed what she'd said. Rolling her eyes, she smacked him lightly on the chest. "You know what I mean."

"Maybe." He slid one hand down her spine then lower, cupping her ass and tugging her so she was flush against his cock. "Because I could also get *behind* this."

Her heart skipped a beat, she bit back a moan.

Then another when his hand kept moving, drifting over the side of her hip, down to grip the outside of her thigh. Hot, *hot* fingers and his eyes—those gorgeous blue eyes—went liquid with desire.

"Max," she breathed.

Those fingers shifted inward, and she inadvertently squeezed her thighs together, wanting them higher, wanting them to slip beneath her underwear and—

"I know," he said, voice rough. "I know."

"When do you—?" She cleared her throat. "When do you think you're going to kiss me again?"

The words had barely crossed her lips before his mouth was on hers. This time, it wasn't a gentle touch. It was demanding and intense and made moisture pool between her thighs. One second, she was turned on and the next, she was weak and shaky with need, desperate for him to be inside her.

She shifted, rubbing herself against his cock, making them both groan in pleasure. Her dress shifted up her legs, exposing the black silk of her panties.

"So fucking sexy," he growled, tearing his mouth away and flipping her in a motion that was so quick she let out a little shriek. Somehow, she ended up with her back against the couch cushions, dress rucked up, legs spread wide, and Max kneeling between her thighs.

Holy fucking shit.

He kissed one ankle then the other, teasing his fingers up

her calves, drifting to the backs of her knees. A nip to the skin just inside her left thigh that made her jump before his tongue darted out to soothe the small hurt, and then he was shifting, dragging his tongue higher and higher until he stopped just on the outside of her panties. He inhaled deeply. "I can't wait to taste this," he said and pressed a kiss against her pussy.

The slight roughness of the lace combined with the damp heat of his mouth sent Angie's desire skyrocketing. She arched off the cushions, gripping Max's hair with both hands, trying to grind closer, to let him taste her.

He steadied her with his hands on her hips, pinning her down onto the couch as he took his time, slowly kissing along the hem of her underwear, occasionally darting his tongue under the lace and teasing her with frustrating little caresses until she was all but ready to tear his hair out, if only that meant he would get his tongue inside her faster.

She pulled, and not too gently.

Max froze, not moving his mouth away from her, the heat of his breath against her pussy an entirely new type of aphrodisiac. He raised one brow.

"Underwear off," she demanded, though the order was weakened by the fact that she was puffing like a locomotive, so she added, "Now."

The smile he shot her should have melted the offending garment right off her thighs. Instead, the only thing it did was make her stomach flutter and more moisture pool between her legs. She could feel the slick heat of her starting to soak through her panties, and apparently Max could as well because he slid a finger over the top of her pussy then held up the glistening digit for her to see.

"So. Fucking. Hot," he told her and sucked it into his mouth.

She'd shuddered at his touch, but when he tasted her? Yeah,

that desire exploded, threatening to incinerate her from the inside out.

Rip.

Angie gasped, the abrasion of lace tearing against her skin made her squirm.

Rip.

Another inhalation and the show of strength as he effortlessly tore the other side had her spreading her thighs, lifting her pelvis toward his mouth.

He grinned, flicked his tongue out for the tiniest tease, and Angie thought he was going to keep on tormenting her, rationing out those little frustrating touches. But then he dove at her, pressing his mouth firmly against her pussy and giving her the best kiss of her life. His tongue circled her clit, firm then gentle, firm then gentle, bringing her higher and higher until he backed off, moving down and thrusting his tongue inside her. The pad of his thumb took over on her clit, and the slightly roughened calluses were a whole new form of torment.

And pleasure.

And torment.

"No," she groaned, lifting her hips, wanting more, *desperate* for more. "I need—"

She broke off, so fucking turned on and yet not exactly knowing what she needed.

But Max seemed to know, even if she didn't understand it herself, because he slipped a finger inside her, tongue and hand switching places, then moved both faster, more firmly until she was writhing on the couch desperate for release.

"Fuck," she huffed. "That's so—"

He slipped a second finger inside her.

She screamed.

He flatted his tongue and circled her clit.

And this time she couldn't scream, the orgasm stole all her

breath, took her ability to speak, to think, to do anything except ride the wave of pleasure all the way down the other side.

Her head plunked back against the couch cushions, white lights flashing behind her lids. "Fuck."

"Mmm." Max's nuzzling made her jump, her eyes darting open.

He had the start of a beard, and the strands had darkened from . . . her.

The sight made that tremble start again, the one low in her stomach, in between her thighs, and her pussy clenched, satisfied and yet not. Because while the orgasm had threatened to burn her to ash, Max still wasn't inside of her.

"My bedroom is just down the hall," she said and not sure that she could navigate the distance in her heels, she bent to slip them off.

His hands gripped hers. "What are you doing?"

"Taking my shoes off."

"They hurting you?"

She frowned, shook her head. Despite them being tall, they were one of the most comfortable pairs of heels she owned. "No."

"Then leave them on."

"Why—?"

The heat in his gaze stopped the rest of her question, and his rapid movement to sweep her up into his arms, pressing her firmly against his chest, the heat of him, the smell, the *power* stole any and all logical thoughts. Especially when he told her, "I want those heels digging into my back as I slide home, Angel. I want you to use them like spurs to prod me like a fucking horse as I pound into you. I want—"

She kissed him as he walked, kissed him as he pushed open the door to her bedroom, kissed him as he tossed her onto the mattress.

Because the words were so fucking hot, but they were also too much.

She needed him *in* her. Now. With less talking.

"Hurry," she said when they finally broke for air and reached into her cleavage to pull out the condom she'd stashed there earlier. "Please, Max. I need you inside me."

He took it from her and ordered, "Turn over."

Angie didn't even consider not obeying, she flipped to her hands and knees, not caring what position Max wanted to take her in, so long as she was taken. But instead of him pushing up her skirt and thrusting home, one palm pressed to the small of her back, coaxing her to lie on her stomach.

The cold metal of the zipper met her skin then started to slowly move down her spine, hot lips trailing in its wake.

"Max—"

"Shh," he murmured. "We have all night."

The zipper stopped just at the top of her ass, and he spread the fabric wide, running those roughened fingertips along her back, making her shiver for the umpteenth time, making her hips shoot up to grind against the hard length of him.

They both groaned at the contact, but Max didn't stop touching her. Instead, he slipped the straps of her dress off her shoulders then gently began massaging the tight muscles along her spine.

"The condom," she said. "You can just—"

"That condom isn't going to fit me, Angel."

"Wh—what?"

"Shh." He chuckled and began kissing down her back, tugging her dress off as he went. She wasn't wearing a bra, and the motion teased her nipples, abrading the hardened points against the cotton. Her breath caught, a moan escaping her lips.

Then the dress was sliding down her hips, over her ankles to land silently on the carpet.

"*Angel.*"

It was curse, benediction, and prayer all in one.

"Max. *Please.*"

"Patience, sweetheart," he said, dropping his hands to her ankles and slowly massaging his way up.

"Are you"—a gasp as those fingers dipped between her thighs—"this focused on the ice?"

A nip to each cheek—and not the ones on her face. "More."

She shuddered when he spread her legs wide and blew a stream of hot air on her center. "I don't think I can survive more," she said, legs trying to close against the wide berth of his shoulders.

His voice was wicked. "Oh, I think you can."

Max licked her, she screamed, and he showed her that she could, in fact, survive more.

TWENTY-FOUR

Max

HE KISSED his way up a limp Angie and gently rolled her to her back.

"Did I kill you?"

Her eyes were closed, her hair a mess, and she'd never been more beautiful. "Uh-huh."

He grinned, gaze drifting down to her chest. "I haven't even gotten to your breasts yet." And they were fucking perfect breasts, round, with perfect-sized nipples that his mouth ached to taste.

She groaned, flopped her head from side to side. "I can't move."

Max chuckled. "You just did."

"Semantics." Her lips curved.

"Just lie back and think of England," he told her, dragging his mouth down her throat and toward her breasts. Fingers slid into his hair, held him in place. "No?"

Her lids peeled back, eyes having darkened to espresso with desire. "I didn't say that."

"Then what *are* you saying?"

"It's not fair you're fully dressed, so get naked first." Angie licked her lips. "*Then* you can kiss me anywhere you want."

Impossibly, Max's cock somehow got harder. "That means I'd have to get off you."

"It means you'd *be naked*."

"Fair point." He pushed off the bed, stripped down in record time, then was back on top of her. Now they were both naked, and it was everything.

"Hi," she said as he cupped her jaw.

He pressed his mouth to hers, pulled back, and smiled. "Hi."

"Kiss me again," she said. "But this time with more tongue."

He laughed, but fuck if he was going to deny her anything, least of all that. And so, he kissed her, sliding his tongue between her lips, moaning when she tangled her tongue with his. Fuck, but she tasted like heaven. Then Angie slid her hand down his chest and grabbed his cock.

Lights flashed behind his lids, a groan bubbled up in his throat, and he thrust his hips forward.

"I can't kiss you," he said, pulling back with another groan, "if you keep doing that."

"You've discovered my evil plan to get your penis in my vagina."

He laughed. Despite the fact that his cock felt as though it would break in half, despite the fact that he was all but shaking with the need to take her, despite his desire to make it so fucking good for Angie—not only because she deserved it, but also because it had been too damned long since he'd slept with a woman and he knew that once he was inside of her, he was at high risk of blowing his load like a seventeen-year-old boy—despite *all* of that, somehow she had him laughing.

"You're amazing," he told her.

"I'm not," she said, then put her fingers over his lips when he would have argued. "I *don't* think I'm special. I'm just . . . me. But I do think it's amazing *you* think of me that way." She paused, head tilting to the side. "Now, that's a lot of thinks."

He grinned. "Now *that* sounds like a line from a Dr. Seuss book."

"Spoken like a single dad—" Her eyes widened as she broke off. "Oh God. I didn't even think of Brayden. Is he going to be okay with—"

He nipped her fingertips still covering his mouth before pressing a kiss there to soothe the tiny hurt. "He asked me to find him a new mom." And then he hurried to add when her eyes widened, presumably in panic, "Not that we're anywhere near there yet. I'm just telling you so you know that he's open to me dating someone."

Her brows pulled down. "Is your ex—?"

"I'm naked, and you have your hand on my cock," he said. "I don't really want to talk about my ex-wife."

Angie's cheeks went pink, and her hand started to let go.

He placed his palm over hers, keeping it in place. "My ex gave up her rights. Just signed them away without a fight. It was shitty and fucked up, but Brayden and I are okay now."

"You're a good dad," she said.

Max shrugged. "I don't know about that. There are so many things I should have done differently, but—"

"It's just you and Brayden, now."

His lips twitched. "And Barf-monster McGee."

"Poor Sparky."

"Poor me," he teased. "I'm naked and hard, and a woman seems to be intent on torturing me."

She stroked her hand up and down the length of him. "Hmm. How can I fix that?"

"I have an idea." He bent, rested his forehead to hers. "But I also want you to know that there's room in our lives for one more. *If* it gets to that point."

Her eyes softened. "Thank you." A pause. "So, can we have sex now?"

He burst out laughing . . . at least until she squeezed him tightly, stroking him from tip to base. *Then* his control vanished, and he forgot all intentions for taking it slow.

After moving his hands to her breasts, he shifted down and let his mouth join the party. That meant her fingers slipped off his cock, but that was okay because he had a mouthful of nipple and that was just as good. It puckered to a hard point as he ran his tongue over and around it, and the way Angie hissed out a breath as he sucked it deep into his mouth had him repeating the process until she moaned and gripped his hair. Then he switched breasts, thrusting a leg between her thighs and groaning as she ground her pussy against him.

Fuck, she was wet.

He licked the underside of one breast and ran the stubble of his beard across her skin, tracing a path with his tongue and mouth, ready to dive back between her thighs and make her come for a third time.

Angie had different ideas.

"So, help me, God. You are going to put on a condom and get inside me, or I will pay off Mandy to dull every pair of skates you own."

He flicked his tongue into her belly button. "You play mean." His fingers slid lower, brushed the top of her pussy.

"*Max.*"

"Fine." He reached for his pants and extracted a condom from his wallet then rolled it on. *Then* he knelt between her thighs and licked her in one long stroke. She cursed, legs flexing, eyes rolling into the back of her head. Her back arched, her hips jumped, and moisture pooled against his tongue.

Only when she was writhing on the mattress, eyes closed tight, breath coming in rapid puffs, and liquid beneath his touch did he rise on his knees and position himself above her.

Then paused.

"Angel," he said.

Dazed eyes opened.

"You sure?"

One long leg hooked around his waist in answer, and he slowly slid home, giving her time to get used to him and attempting to wrestle the urge to pound into her under control.

Her hips shifted, encouraging him to move.

He pulled out, pushed back in, loving the way her lips formed a little O, loving the soft moans as he moved.

"More," she said. "Max, *baby*, I need you—"

Fuck. He loved that she called him baby.

He moved a little faster, sliding in and out but in a measured pace, not wanting to hurt her, not wanting this to be anything but good for her.

Sweat dripped down his spine, pleasure coiled in his dick, spread outwards throughout his entire body, hampering his rhythm, wanting him to move faster, harder, *deeper*.

But he forced himself to stay steady, to go slow . . . at least until Angie wrapped her other leg around him and demanded, "Fuck me, Max. Hard."

And then the leash snapped.

He pounded into her, driving them both up and up and up until Angie screamed and clenched around his cock and finally —thank fuck but, *finally*—he exploded.

The orgasm was torn from him, locking his spine, fire shooting down his limbs before pleasure engulfed every single nerve and his vision went black.

Max came back to awareness on top of Angie.

He was limp with pleasure and no doubt heavy as fuck, but

when he tried to shift off her, not wanting to crush her, she closed her arms around his shoulders and murmured, "Not yet. Just . . . just a little longer."

Kissing her shoulder, her jaw, her cheek, he nodded and stayed in place, feeling both sliced open and totally vulnerable, and yet . . . finding there was no place he'd rather be.

Angie. His Angel.

Without even trying, she'd managed to stitch herself right into his heart.

And Max found that he didn't mind the feeling one bit.

TWENTY-FIVE

Angie

"HI!" She sat down at the table across from Mandy, coffee in hand and happy to have a break from the office. Her department had six projects running concurrently, which meant Angie was basically juggling knives and axes and flamethrowers, all at the same time.

Oh, and maybe a chainsaw or two along with them.

No big deal.

Her sister smiled. "Hi, yourself. You okay? You look like you've been pulled backward through a bush."

Angie's eyes widened. "Dad used to say that."

"Oh"—Mandy's breath caught—"I'd forgotten."

Angie reached up and attempted to smooth her hair then stopped with a shrug and a laugh. "And, he'd probably say me attempting to make myself presentable after the morning I had would be like putting lipstick on a pig," Angie said.

"Yeah. He would have." A pause. "Also, this just in: Dad was an jerk."

Angie snorted. "Yup."

"Anyway, old news aside, I'm guessing by the wrinkled clothes and messy ponytail that work has been crazy for you, too?" Mandy asked and when Angie nodded, added, "Thanks for taking the time out to meet me. I feel like things have been nuts with the long road trip and then Blane and I moving in together."

"Work *has* been insane, but just with the usual stuff," she said. "How's the house hunting been going?"

They talked for the next little while, each of them sipping their coffees and nibbling on the yummy apple tarts that this particular bakery was known for. They'd been trying to get together a few times each week for lunch or coffee and had discovered a shared love for all apple pastries as well as a hatred for romaine lettuce and sweet tea. The house hunt hadn't been easy, especially in the competitive Bay Area, and they spent a few minutes discussing neighborhoods and school choices before getting into the non-secret work projects that Angie could discuss.

Her phone buzzed just as she started sharing a story about hanging with Kelsey and company at Bobby's and the "little barely-legal"—Cora's words, not Angie's—who'd tried to pick up Kels with a horribly sleazy line. Angie glanced down at her cell to see a text from Max and felt a huge smile break out on her face.

"Max?" Mandy asked.

Angie nodded. "Yes. He's just . . ."

"Special."

Another nod, but this time followed by Angie biting her lip. "I really like him. I didn't think it was possible after Dad and the contract and the assault. I just thought I would always be gun shy and that I was destined to be alone."

"But you and Max are different."

"Yeah."

"You realize I do have to ask you what you meant by 'contract'," Mandy said. "And attack, for that matter."

Angie blew out a breath. "I know."

She'd promised herself that if she were going to try and have a relationship with Mandy that she had to be open and honest about everything. As painful and uncomfortable as it was, Angie knew it was the only way forward—for their relationship and for *her* chance at a happy future.

She wouldn't be the shameful secret.

Not any longer.

And if by a slim chance, the contract did become an issue, Angie had never touched the money that came along with it. Until recently, she hadn't understood why she hadn't spent it, but now she knew.

Yes, things had sometimes been tight.

But she'd recognized the myriad of strings attached to that payout. They were as heavy as giant steel chains and thankfully, or maybe *luckily*, she hadn't wanted to shoulder that burden.

So now, older and hopefully wiser, Angie was damned glad she'd left that money alone.

Mandy reached across the table and touched her hand. "You don't have to."

"Have to what?"

"Share any of it," Mandy said. "I'll ask because I care and because I want to know you, but you don't owe me anything, Angie. I'm just so glad to have you here now." She smiled sadly. "I always felt so alone as a kid. Isolated and just not wanted, and I would have given anything for a sister. I feel so lucky to have that chance now."

"Shit." Angie pulled her hand free and glanced down at the table.

"Um, did I overstep?"

She blinked, turned her gaze back to Mandy. "No. I'm"—she sniffed—"I promised myself I wouldn't cry."

"Oh." Her sister dashed a finger under each eye. "Try being pregnant. The waterworks are fucking ridiculous. I can't even hear the first notes of those SPCA commercials without bursting into tears." She rolled her eyes. "Yesterday, Blane bought me an organizer for all of my tape, and I sobbed for a good fifteen minutes. I swear, an alien has taken over my body."

Angie raised a finger. "First, the animal commercials are sad as hell so I feel you, and second, you need an organizer for tape?"

Mandy waved a hand. "There are so many types—athletic, plastic, scotch, stick, KT, paper—and those are just what my baby-addled brain can think of. I'm sure I missed some that I use on a daily basis. I was complaining about how they kept shifting around in the drawer, stopping it from opening normally and he"—she blinked—"bought me one. And now, *look*, I'm crying about tape again."

"Sorry." Angie bit back a smile.

"No, you're not."

"That's true."

She and Mandy looked at each other and started laughing.

"Thanks for pestering me and continuing to reach out," Angie said, once they'd stopped. "I was so wrapped up in my life, in protecting myself, that my life was empty. You prompted me to take those first baby steps into getting out of my own head."

Along with Max and Kelsey pushing her, of course.

But that first email from Mandy the previous year had created those hairline fractures in her protective shell, had made her wonder *what if*, rather than *what could happen*.

"I'm so glad I found out about you," Mandy told her. "I'm just sorry it wasn't sooner."

"You want to know the really sad part?"

Mandy bit her lip. "Do I?"

"Maybe not." Angie sighed. "But I think in the spirit of building an open relationship, I should tell you two things." She took a sip of her coffee, delaying for just a moment longer before finally blurting. "I knew about you. I knew you existed my whole life."

Mandy's jaw dropped open. "But how? No, *why?* Why didn't you—?" She broke off, staring at Angie with hurt eyes.

"I should have reached out. I really regret that I didn't, but I just—"

Angie swallowed hard.

"What?"

She shook her head.

Mandy laced her fingers with hers. "Just what, Ang?"

"I hated you." Mandy recoiled, trying to pull back, but Angie gripped her fingers tight. "No. That's not what I meant. I mean, I was hurt. Dad would come to our place and tell me the reason he couldn't see me was because of you and your mom and that it was your guys' fault that he couldn't be there more." She sighed. "I was young and didn't understand he was trying to manipulate me, and then he got into the accident and I saw *you* on TV with him and not me, and I just . . ."

"Hated me."

Mandy's voice was dead, icy-cold, and Angie flinched, wondering if she'd just ruined everything. She shouldn't have said that, shouldn't have risked hurting her sister. "I didn't know the bigger picture. I'm sorry. I should have—"

Mandy pulled her hand free and jumped to her feet.

And Angie's heart clenched.

She'd fucked it all up, screwed up her chance to have a sister. Throat tight, she dropped her gaze to the table. Why had she suggested the coffee shop? Now she was going to be a sobbing mess, sitting alone with a half-finished espresso growing cold.

In other words: pathetic.

A hand on her arm made her startle, eyes flying up.

Mandy was kneeling by her side. "I'm going to hug you now. Brace yourself."

Angie croaked out a laugh. "Okay."

They embraced tightly, sniffing and Angie knew she wasn't the only one blinking back tears. "Our dad was a real fucking asshole, wasn't he?" Mandy asked, still hugging her.

Angie nodded. "That he was."

Mandy shifted and Angie let her go. "You're going to hurt your knees. You should sit down."

Her sister waggled her brows. "Blane likes it when I kneel."

"*Ew*."

Mandy dragged her chair over near Angie's. "Sorry. I had to."

Angie wrinkled her nose, took another sip of coffee. "Yeah, I don't think you *had* to tell me you like to give your fiancé blow jobs."

"Maybe." She took a seat. "But at least we're not crying now."

Angie chuckled. "True."

They sat in silence for a few minutes, both of their gazes on the busy coffee shop, but no doubt their minds were on their respective pasts and their fucked-up parentage. "So, despite the risk of having more tears, I do have to gently probe about the assault. Are you okay? Is there someone I need to have killed?"

"Sadly, the attack is almost easier for me to talk about than the contract. I was nearly raped on a dark street corner. I was naïve, didn't know how to protect myself, and though the man hurt me, the assault was stopped by a Good Samaritan." She inhaled and exhaled slowly. "He did—you know—get inside me, but only with his fingers. They stopped him before it got worse."

Mandy's face was pale, and she pushed her coffee away. "I'm so sorry that happened to you."

"Me, too. For a long time, I couldn't even stand the most casual touch from a man, but Max . . . he's different. He makes me feel different inside." A shrug. "Not broken, I guess. Almost normal."

Mandy smiled.

"I just feel like my heart has known him my whole life," she said. "Almost from the beginning, I've trusted him, deep down and with every fiber of my soul."

"Poetry trust." Mandy nodded sagely.

Angie's brows drew together. "What?"

"You have poetry trust with him. You know, like when you find someone in your life—it can be a friend or lover or spouse—that gets you so effortlessly that you could write sappy poems to them." Mandy shrugged. "Blane was that for me. My heart recognized him for what he was almost before my body did and *way* as fuck before my mind accepted him. You too, you know. It's why I kept emailing and holding out hope. I didn't know you from anyone on the street, but I just felt like I had to keep trying or my life would be . . ."

"Missing something."

Mandy nodded. "Yes. That."

"Thank you for not giving up on me."

"Shush," Mandy told her. "You already said that."

Angie grinned. "Okay then, if you don't want my gratitude then at least tell me what my sappy poem would be."

"Hmm." Mandy's eyes focused on the ceiling as she pondered. "Okay, I've got it. Sister, Sister. I'm your sister. We're from the same mister but another sister—*aw fuck*." She burst out laughing. "Ang, I've got no idea what your sappy poem might be, but I'm glad you're here now."

Angie was giggling so hard it was hard to get any words out. "Me . . . too . . ."

Mandy made a bowing gesture with her hand. "Sister from the Same Mister. An Amanda Shallows exclusive."

And then they were both cracking up again.

Eventually they regained control. Mandy took a sip of her coffee, said, "I'm so happy you guys found each other. Max has had some tough years, and he and Brayden deserve someone as special as you."

"Dammit," Angie said, tone accusatory. "See? Now you're going to make me cry again. Horrible poetry is better. "

"Heaven help me," Mandy said. "Quick. Tell me something that annoys you so I can play the condescending older sister role. I know!" She raised a finger. "You need me to give you relationship advice or scold you and tell you that you can't borrow my clothes"—she wrinkled her nose—"except we're close to the same size, and I think that would be kind of fun."

Angie snorted. "Ha, girlfriend. This ass won't fit into those jeans of yours. We can trade T-shirts."

"*My* ass is going to be gigantic. But your shirts *are* the best, though," she replied. "That mashup one you have with the avocado and the cat. It's so cute."

"I can admit that I have a T-shirt addiction." Angie popped the last bite of apple turnover into her mouth. "It's bad. Between that and flannel and *Star Wars*, maybe like five percent of my clothing can be considered adult?" She laughed. "And that portion is all work-related."

"Hey, as far as I'm concerned, that's pretty good." Mandy's own phone buzzed. "I only survive because ninety percent of my clothes are Gold-issued uniform shirts and pants."

"You need to get that?" Angie asked.

She shook her head. "Just my ten-minute reminder so I leave in time. Pregnancy brain is real, yo."

"Excuses, excuses." Angie dodged the smack Mandy directed her way. "Sister abuse!" she teased.

"Not hardly." But Mandy was grinning.

Angie drained her coffee. "So, if we only have ten minutes, should I tell you the last of it?"

It was the only piece left . . . not to confess, exactly, but to air out?

No. That wasn't right. It was more like . . . the final portion that had power over her and her relationship with Mandy. Because it hadn't just been her anxiety that had kept her from forging ties with her sister, but—

"The contract?" Mandy asked.

"Yeah." Angie sighed. "Except, it's not really a contract. I call it that in my head because it felt very much like one, but really it has to do with Dad's Will."

Mandy's brows drew together as she reached for her coffee and took a sip.

"I mean, there *were* legal documents involved—my mom and I had to sign NDAs in order to see what he left us in the Will, and I *did* sign one and was of age when I did, so . . . but that's not the part that made things so difficult." She exhaled, tried to steady her words, her thoughts. "Things got screwed up because the Will stated that in order for me or my mom to inherit anything, I could never have a relationship with you." She shook her head. "I didn't understand that the two documents were separate until my mom died and her lawyer sent me her papers. And I couldn't bring myself to even look at her things until last year. She was all I had, and—"

"I'm sorry."

Angie smiled at her sister. "For the longest time, I thought if

I talked to you or reached out to you that I could be sued and that I'd lose—"

"Everything."

"Yeah." She swallowed. "Then you emailed, and I went through my mom's things and read everything and realized that I *could* maybe have a sister. My mom wasn't around to be put at risk. Dad was gone"—a sigh—"but that wasn't what held me back."

"What did?" Mandy asked.

"I was scared. Pathetic, I know," she said. "But I was too scared to reach out—or really, even to reach halfway—" She broke off, struggling to find the right words.

Mandy squeezed her hand. "I understand being scared—we Shallows girls have all sorts of trust issues. But I guess my question is why be scared of me? We had no history and I was initiating the relationship, I was the one putting myself out there . . . so what made you so nervous?"

Angie bit her lip then decided to tell the truth. "I thought you'd hate me. I thought that if I put myself out there and you got to know me that you'd change your mind."

Yo-yoed from one extreme to the next, like their father.

"Is that why you left the day Blane and I got engaged?"

Angie considered that. "Yes. Though, truthfully, I can say it was only part of the reason." A shrug. "I can't say me leaving was totally altruistic because it wasn't. I was beyond anxious, yes, worried you'd hate me, and, I know it sounds lame, but I also didn't want to ruin your special day."

Mandy shook her head. "It *is* lame." She took a bite of her pastry, chewed, and swallowed. "Because you would have only made it better," she said. "But I do get it. Thank you for being considerate."

"I was part of the other family. It was the least I could—"

"*No.*" Angie blinked at her sister's tone. "You're *my* family now. Our parents can all suck it. They were twisted assholes who enjoyed hurting each other—well, I don't know about your mom—"

One half of Angie's mouth curved. "She can definitely be considered an asshole."

"Okay. Good." A pause as Mandy considered that. "Well, not good exactly, but good that *all* our parents are assholes?" She shook her head. "Shit. That sounds—"

"Accurate," Angie interjected.

Mandy giggled. "Yes. That's true. Okay, so we were surrounded by assholes growing up, but now we've found each other and—"

"We can be assholes together?"

"You're the worst."

Angie grinned. "How about we can be well-adjusted and move forward in productive, happy lives?"

"Better," Mandy said.

"Or maybe, we can just be sisters?"

Mandy sniffed before resting her head on Angie's shoulder. "Okay, that'll do."

TWENTY-SIX

Monday

MAX: I miss you.

Angie: You've been gone for one day.

Max: Maybe, but I still miss you.

Angie: So needy.

Max: Ouch.

Angie: I'm kidding. I miss you too.

Max: Yeah?

Angie: Don't go fishing for compliments now.

Max: *puppy dog eyes GIF*

Angie: Nice try. You already know you're both adorable and hot.

Max: Not sure that combination works for me.

Angie: Well, it sure as hell works for me. *fanning herself GIF*

Max: *waggling eyebrows GIF*

Angie: Goodnight, Max. Good game tonight.

Max: Night, Angel.

Tuesday

Max: Do you want to come over for dinner on Friday and meet Brayden officially?

    Angie: . . .

Max: No pressure.

    Angie: Is Brayden ready for that?

Max: He'll love you. Sparky will too.

    Angie: Does Sparky like cats?

Max: Supposedly.

    Angie: Hmm.

Max: I'll order in Chinese.

    Angie: You had to go and tempt me with fried rice, didn't you?

Max: Frankly, I'm tempting myself. This diet that the nutritionist has us on is torture.

    Angie: Poor, spoiled hockey players.

    Angie: Don't you dare send that puppy dog eyes GIF

Max: *puppy dog eyes GIF*

    Angie: OMG. You're the worst.

Max: Does this mean you're coming to dinner?

    Angie: . . .

Max: Please?

    Angie: I'll see you at your place on Friday.

Wednesday

Angie: Thank you so much! I love it.

    Max: I'm so glad they came.

    Angie: They're adorable and thank you for sending them to my apartment and not my office. It'd be a little hard to explain why I was receiving *Star Wars* underwear at my desk.

    Max: I was tempted, I have to admit.

Angie: *squinty eyes GIF*

Max: You'll also notice this gift was confetti free.

Angie: That will not go unnoticed on Friday evening.

Max: It might have to be Saturday morning.

Angie: Huh?

Max: Brayden.

Angie: Oh. Duh. I'm sorry, I'm new to this.

Max: Do you mind?

Angie: What? No! Of course not. You guys are a package deal, and he's a wonderful kid. I'm looking forward to getting to know him better. I just . . .

Max: What?

Angie: I hope he doesn't hate me.

Max: Impossible.

Angie: . . .

Max: He also has a playdate on Saturday morning, so you can demonstrate your undying affection for non-confetti gifts at that time.

Angie: Trying to distract me?

Max: He'll love you, Angel. It's impossible for anyone not to.

Max: Now, it's late for you. Get some sleep and we'll talk tomorrow.

Thursday night

Max: Hopping on the plane, will be really late getting home.

Angie: Have a safe flight. I can't believe how much I've missed you this week.

Max: Because I'm totally miss-able.

Angie: So pun-tastic.

Max: I'll have you know, Blue just asked why I lol-ed.

Angie: What'd you tell him?

Max: That a beautiful woman has me by the balls.

Angie: I'm not sure if I'm intrigued or disgusted.

Max: Story of my life.

Max: And you're definitely intrigued, sweetheart. Just btw. ;)

Max: Gotta turn off my cell. See you tomorrow.

Angie: Your place at 7 pm. Can't wait.

Max: Goodnight, Angel. Sleep tight.

TWENTY-SEVEN

Max

MAX TURNED TO BRAYDEN, who was sprawled out on his bed. "Hey, bud?

"Yeah?" His son had his nose in his iPad.

"I have a friend coming over for dinner. Chinese okay?"

"Yup." He pressed a few things on the screen. "Is it Blue?"

Max sank onto the edge of the bed, hit pause on the game, and waited for Brayden to look up at him. "You remember Angie? From the vet's office?"

Brayden's eyebrows dragged together. "With the cat?"

"Yeah. Well, you know Mandy, right?" A nod. "It turns out that Angie is her sister."

Those brows relaxed. "Oh, okay." He sounded disappointed.

"You okay?" Max asked.

Brayden reached for the iPad, sighing when Max set it on the other side of him. "I'm fine."

Considering the amount of mope in that statement, Brayden *wasn't* fine. Shit. Had he misread things with Brayden horribly?

Was his son not ready for him to be in a relationship? Max's gut churned at the thought. Fuck, because Angie was—

"I just thought that maybe Angie might not be your friend."

Max froze, tried to puzzle that one out. "You don't want us to be friends?"

"Well, I like Mandy, and she's your friend."

"Okaaay."

"And Angie's your friend, too, right?" Brayden seemed to be holding his breath as he waited for Max's answer.

"Yes, of course she is."

Brayden's face fell. "Oh."

"I'm not following, bud. Why does that make you sad?"

His son sighed. "Because if you only ever have friends, I'll never get a new mom, and you'll never have a new wife." Tears shone in Brayden's eyes. "And then you'll never be happy."

"Hey, come here." He tugged his son close. "First, I love you. You're the best thing that has ever happened to me, and I am so happy to have you in my life. If it was just you and me forever, that would be okay."

"Really?"

"Really, *really*." Max ran a hand through Brayden's hair. "Second. Angie is a friend, but I'd also like her to be more. If you're okay with it."

Startled blue eyes met his. "Like a girlfriend?"

"Yeah," he said. "Is that okay with you?"

Brayden smiled. "She had a really nice smile, and her cat was cute."

The top two reasons to want to date a woman: a nice smile and a cute puss—

Max snorted. "Yeah, bud. She did."

"Do you love her?" Brayden asked.

"Of course, I do."

Four words emerging unbidden from Max's lips that made

him freeze in place, four words that he'd never really considered, but also four words that settled into his brain, his heart, his soul.

He loved Angie.

Of course, he did.

"Cool." Brayden reached for his iPad, un-paused the game. "Can we get sweet and sour chicken?"

"Yeah, bud," Max said, pulling out his cell to order the food.

───────

THERE WAS a knock on the door just as Max was shrugging into a fresh shirt. It was a few minutes before seven, so it was either the food or Angie.

"Don't answer that," he called to Brayden, who'd pushed up from the bed and looked as though he'd sprint down the stairs. "Remember? You should have an adult answer the door unless you know who it is."

"Isn't that your friend?"

"Maybe," Max agreed. "But better to be sure, yeah?"

Brayden considered that before nodding. "Yeah."

Max finished buttoning his shirt just as the bell peeled again. "Let's go see if that's food or Angie."

Brayden ran in front of him, pounding down the stairs and skidding to a stop.

"Can I open it now?" he asked when Max was five steps from the bottom.

"Yeah," Max said, smiling.

That smile faded as soon as Brayden turned the knob and pulled open the door.

Because it wasn't Angie or the person from DoorDash with their food.

It was Suzanne.

"Fuck," he muttered, rushing down the stairs to stand between Brayden and his ex. "What are you doing here?" Yes, his tone was frosty, but what the fuck? The last time they'd spoken on the phone, he'd made it clear—

"You said I could come home," Suzanne said . . . or rather whined.

Apparently, he hadn't made it clear.

"Brayden," he said quietly, "can you please go play in your room for a few minutes."

"Can I have a hug, baby?" Suzanne asked, when their son turned to leave.

Brayden looked at Max. "Your body, your choice, bud," he said.

Relief poured over Brayden's face. Then without another look back, he ran up the stairs.

"He—" Suzanne's eyes glittered with tears.

And Max was too cynical by now to believe they were anything but a show.

"You can't show up here like this," he said. "You gave up that right when you signed the papers."

"Brayden is my son."

"*Our* son, though you seemed to forget that when you sped the fuck out of town," Max grit out. He forced himself to stop, to breathe and calm his tone. "I won't have you upsetting Brayden."

"I miss him." Her lip trembled, those tears escaped.

"I said, we could work something out," Max told her. "That we'd find a way for you to live close and still have a relationship with Brayden. But showing up on my front porch unannounced isn't the way. Move somewhere nearby, get to know your son again slowly—"

"I know my son!" she snapped. "I carried him in *my* body. I pushed him out of my fucking vagina, and I have the goddamned stretch marks to prove it."

Suzanne was right. She'd done all those things.

But that didn't mean she was a mother. Mothers didn't leave. Mothers didn't abandon their children.

"You haven't seen or talked to him in almost two years."

"That's not fair—"

"What's his favorite food?"

"Mac and cheese."

Max shook his head. "Nope. His best friend at school?"

"Kevin."

"Kevin moved away last year."

"How would I know that?" she growled then shrugged. "The kid was an idiot anyway."

Max clenched one hand into a fist, pressing it to his thigh, and striving for patience. "What about his favorite color?"

"Blue."

Max sighed. "No, Suzanne. It's green now," he said. "It's been a long time. Things change."

"Not *all* things change, Maxie." She drifted close, breasts brushing against his chest. "*We* didn't change. We always were really good together—"

He gripped her wrists and stepped back. "Don't."

A throat cleared.

His stomach sank when he saw who it was.

Angie stood behind them, the bag of food in her hands. "Hi," she said, glancing between him and Suzanne.

Well, this was the moment she was going to run.

She'd caught him with Suzanne all but plastered to his chest, and she was going to run. *Fuck.* He'd just discovered that he loved her, and his ex-wife had torpedoed any chance of a future.

"Hi," he said, still holding Suzanne's wrists as she actively tried to sidle closer, trying to stake some sort of claim she didn't have a chance in hell of possessing.

Angie's eyes softened slightly.

Or maybe he was going crazy with hope.

"Hi," she repeated, eyes searching his.

"Hi," he replied, gaze pleading that she understand.

"You already said that," Suzanne snapped, jerking both of their stares back to her. "Now leave me and my husband alone—"

"*Ex*," Angie interjected.

"What?" Suzanne asked.

"*Ex*-husband." Angie slipped past Suzanne, paused at his side, and rose on tiptoe to press a kiss to his mouth. "I'll get the food set up in the kitchen."

"It's down—"

"I can manage." She kissed him again. "Nice to meet you," she said to Suzanne. "Max and I look forward to seeing you around."

Suzanne gasped. "I—"

Angie didn't wait for the rest of the reply, just took the food into the kitchen. He listened to her move around the space, heard a few drawers open and close, and knew that she'd be fine for a few minutes.

"Things change," he said into the silence. "*I* changed."

"I thought—"

"That I'd just wait around like a pathetic puppy?" He saw the expression on Suzanne's face. "*You* left," he said. "I fought for you, for us, for Brayden, but you just left."

"I wasn't happy." Tears trailed down her cheeks.

"I'm sorry, Suzanne, but that doesn't matter. Life gets hard and twisted and fucked up, and real relationships can weather that, but only if both parties stay and fight." No longer having to actively hold her back from him, he released her wrists. "You didn't fight for us, or me, or Brayden. You left."

"I made a mistake."

He shook his head. "It's too late."

"I miss you."

"No," he said. "You miss being taken care of, you miss the money and the stability, but you don't miss me."

"No, that's not true. I *do* miss you," she whined. "We were good together, and I miss—"

Max nudged her out the door, started to close it. "Here's a hint. The person you *should* be missing is Brayden," he said. "Not me. Because he's the only one you have a chance with. And if you screw up again or wait too long, I think that chance will disappear, too."

Click.

He locked the door, leaned back against it, and sighed.

"You okay?"

Angie.

He glanced up, saw the beautiful woman who had stolen his heart looking at him with so much compassion and concern that he couldn't hold back the words. "I love you."

Her jaw dropped open. "What?"

He crossed over to her, took her fingers in his. "I should have probably waited more than thirty seconds after slamming the door on my ex to tell you, but . . ."

She bit her lip. "You love me?"

Max nodded. "I do."

Those pale brown eyes warmed, her mouth curved. "Oh." She spun back to the kitchen. "Well, the food is going to get cold—"

He slid an arm around her waist. "You're more worried about the food getting cold than me telling you that I love you?"

Angie shrugged. "Priorities."

He poked a finger in the spot on her side that he'd discovered was ticklish. "Food over love?"

She giggled. "Yup—" A little shriek as she whirled in his arms, grabbing his hand to halt the tickling. "I'm kidding"—a gasp—"I'm just kidding. I—uh—love—*Stop!*—you, too."

"Lies," he said, but stilled his hand.

Angie was pressed against him, breathing hard, and Max found that his own pulse picked up, that he was suddenly breathing hard, too. But then again, that was his body on Angie. She was nearby, and he was hard.

It was as simple as that.

"You love me?" she asked.

"Yeah."

"Damn," she said. "You do realize that means you're stuck with me now, don't you?"

He brushed a strand of her hair back, tucked it behind one ear. "I think I can handle it." He pressed his lips to hers, stole a kiss. "You think you can handle us?"

"I—"

"Dad!" Brayden shouted. "Sparky's not in his crate!" The words reached them the same moment there was a huge crash in the kitchen

Max rolled his eyes heavenward. "What about now?" he asked. "Think you can handle us now?"

Angie huffed out a laugh. "Hell, no, but I'm looking forward to trying."

Max stole one more kiss. "Me, too, Angel. Me, too."

He led the way into the kitchen, took one look at the mess Sparky had made of the containers and plates Angie had so nicely laid out on the table, sighed, then pulled out his phone to order more Chinese.

Life got messy sometimes . . . but thank God for DoorDash.

TWENTY-EIGHT

Angie

"ANGIE?"

She tore her eyes from the ice—the Gold were down by a goal with less than five minutes left in the third period—to look at Brayden, who was sitting in the stands next to her. "What's up, bud?"

"Will you come to my concert at school?"

Her heart skipped a beat. This kid was just so sweet. "Of course, bud. When is it?"

"Next Tuesday at ten."

She pulled out her phone. "I'm putting it in my calendar right now."

"Cool." He turned his face back to the game, but not before she saw his mouth curve up into a smile.

It had been two weeks since that night at Max's house, when Angie had stumbled onto Suzanne and Max's disagreement. Well, Angie didn't really know what to characterize it as —a disagreement, Suzanne coming on to Max, unfinished business—because Max had brushed her off, saying it wasn't a big deal and that he'd passed the information on to his lawyer to care of.

Meanwhile, she and Max had managed to squeeze in two other nights at her apartment when Brayden had sleepovers at his friends' houses.

Those moments had been glorious, Max somehow showing so much focus between the sheets that Angie was often surprised she didn't glance down and find she'd been reduced to ash.

But that was how she was with Max—reduced to pieces yet put back together stronger.

Herself . . . only a better version.

She smiled, feeling content and relaxed in a way she'd never imagined possible. The last few weeks had been filled with lunch dates with Mandy plus a few nights out with her friends, and, of course, Max and Brayden—she'd even gotten to watch one of Brayden's soccer games before they'd gone out for pizza. Somehow, she'd gone from being alone to having a sister and friends and . . . she was part of a family.

"Go, Dad!"

Angie blinked and focused back on the ice. Sure enough, Max had the puck on his stick and was skating up the ice. She held her breath as he crossed the blue line and dished off a pass to Blue—just thirty seconds left in the game. Blue barreled toward the net, raised his stick to shoot, and . . .

Passed back to Max.

Who slammed it home.

Holy—

She shot to her feet and screamed at the top of her lungs, everyone in the arena mirroring the movement, including Brayden, who was jumping up and down and cheering like crazy.

"That was *my* Dad!" he shouted.

"Yes, it was." She high-fived him then blinked when

Brayden wrapped his arms around her and squeezed tight. And when she hugged him back, it was the most natural action in the world.

"That goal was awesome," he said when the celebration wound down and they took their seats again.

"It *was* awesome," she agreed, turning her attention back to the ice as both teams lined up to for a face-off. A few seconds later, the buzzer sounded, signaling the end of regulation.

Brayden fist-pumped. "Overtime!"

"Yup," Angie said, smiling as the teams congregated near their coaches for a quick discussion. "Let me just text Anna and let her know that the game is running later than we expected."

This was the first time Angie had been alone with Brayden, and because Max was leaving straight after the game for a flight to L.A. with the team, Anna was going to meet them at the arena to take Brayden home.

It's getting late, she said when Anna told her that she hadn't left yet. *Do you want me to meet you at Max's, so you don't have to wait or deal with traffic?*

That would be great, actually, Anna replied. *I need to get Brayden's stuff ready for school in the morning.*

I'll text you when we're leaving.

"Okay, bud," Angie said, ruffling his hair as the ref blew his whistle and both teams moved to line up for the puck drop. "I'll drive you home once the game is over. Anna will meet us there."

"'Kay." He didn't take his eyes from the ice.

And it was a good thing, too, because with a reduced number of players—three per side instead of five—the game moved like lightning. The Gold got a quick chance right off the face-off, but then the puck took a weird bounce and suddenly it was a two on none heading the other way.

Meaning, Brit, the Gold's goalie, was facing two opponents, with no help from her teammates.

Angie bit back a curse.

But then, out of the corner of her eye, she saw a flash of black, watched as one of the Gold streaked back into their end.

And dove headfirst into the play.

The puck came across on a pass, bounced off the player's helmet, and deflected into the corner. Somehow, she knew it was Max before he jumped to his feet and chased after it, tipping it up to Stefan, who passed it up to Blue.

The Kings—their opponent that night—seemed stunned by the rapid turn and that heartbeat of hesitation gave the Gold the opportunity they needed. Blue carried the puck up and, in a move that was so fast Angie's eyes had a hard time tracking it, froze the goalie in place before casually sliding the puck home on the far side of the goal.

"Holy—" She smothered the curse just in time.

Because that had been a hell of a goal.

"That was dirty," Brayden shouted over the cheering.

Angie laughed. Max had just explained to them earlier, that dirty didn't always mean what she'd thought it did—a cheap shot or underhanded play. Nope, sometimes dirty could mean *really* good.

And that goal had been *really* good.

"You're absolutely right, bud. That goal definitely was *dirty*." She glanced out onto the ice and saw Max was looking at them. "Brayden." She nudged him, pointing at the Gold's bench, where Max had paused before going into the locker room. "Your dad."

Brayden grinned and waved. "Dad!"

Max waved back then pointed at her and touched the space above his heart.

Angie melted. This man.

She loved him so much.

Brayden was jumping around, jazzed from the game's

ending, and Max waved one more time before disappearing back into the hallway.

They'd said their goodbyes to Max before the game, considering the team's flight and the fact that it was a school night for Brayden, so she and Bray slowly made their way out of the crowded arena.

"Hey! Angie!" Kelsey's voice stopped her.

"Hey! I didn't think you were coming tonight. Brayden"—she touched his shoulder—"This is my friend from work, Kelsey."

Brayden waved. "Hi."

Kels smiled. "Hi, Brayden." To Angie she said, "Devon talked me into it."

"Are you Devon Scott?" Brayden's voice was awe-filled.

Devon squatted next to Brayden. "Hi, bud. Yes, I am."

"This is Brayden Montgomery," Angie told him.

"Wow," Devon said. "Your dad had a heck of a game tonight."

The compliment lit up Brayden's face. "He was awesome!"

"He's better than Devon was," Kelsey stage-whispered.

Brayden giggled, and he and Devon fist-bumped before Devon stood. "It's getting late," he said. "Do you guys need a ride anywhere?"

Angie shook her head. "Thanks, but no. We're just in the lot outside."

They said their goodbyes then left the arena. The space always emptied out quickly, but tonight they seemed to be on the tail end of things, and she could see there were only a few cars still parked in the lot across the street. It was darker than she expected, and Angie regretted not taking Devon up on his offer of a ride.

This was bringing up some unpleasant memories.

And anxieties. And—

Brayden grabbed her hand, making her jump, but Angie forced herself to swallow her nerves and smile down at him. "Are you tired?" she asked.

"No way." He sped his way down the sidewalk, almost dragging her along in the process. "I could stay up for hours—" Except that statement was punctuated by a giant yawn, and she had the feeling he was about to crash and burn on the car ride home.

"It was an exciting game for sure," she told him. "Thanks for hanging out with me."

"I can't believe you asked. Or that Dad let me go."

They'd paused at the crosswalk, waiting for the signal to change. "Because it was late?"

"Yeah."

The light turned. "But why were you surprised I asked?"

He shrugged, eyes down on the ground and Angie tensed because this wasn't her expertise. What if she said the wrong thing and hurt his feelings? Or overstepped and—

She was just going to tell him what was in her heart.

Squatting next to him once they'd crossed the road, she said. "I *like* hanging out with you, Brayden. I've really cherished getting to know you the last few weeks."

He paused, tilted his head. "You really mean that?"

Angie squeezed his shoulder. "I really do." A pause. "And I hope you don't mind me hanging out with you and your dad."

"No. You're pretty cool."

"Just pretty?" she teased, standing again. "Coming from a super cool seven-year-old like you, I'll take it."

"You should," he said sagely. "I am really cool."

Angie laughed. "Coolness aside, it's a school night and it's late, even for a wicked cool boy like yourself."

He groaned but led the way to her car.

She unlocked it, watched to make sure he buckled himself correctly into his booster seat.

"Angie?" he asked, just as she was about to close the door.

"Yeah, bud?"

"Can we go to another game together sometime?"

There her heart went again, expanding, opening up to let this kid deep inside. "I'd like that, Brayden."

He nodded, playing it cool. "'kay."

"'Kay." She closed the door, smothering a grin.

A movement out of the corner of her eye had her whipping around on a gasp.

Crack.

Everything went black.

TWENTY-NINE

Max

THE CALL CAME JUST as he was about to get on the bus to take them to the airport.

Frowning, he glanced down at the screen, saw it was Anna, and hurried to pick up.

"Hello?"

"Max?" she said, breathing heavy. "Are you still at the arena?"

His gut twisted. "Yes."

"You need to get out to Lot C. That's where Angie and Brayden were parked, and there's been . . . an incident."

"What kind of *incident?*" he asked.

Bernard was right behind him in line but took one look at Max's face and stepped to the side. "Go," he told him.

Max nodded and started sprinting around the building, heart pounding. "Anna," he snapped. "What happened—?" But by then he'd made it around to the front of the arena, saw the flashing lights, and the question stopped in his throat.

He barely checked for cars as he ran across the street. Anna was kneeling on the ground next to . . . Angie.

An officer tried to stop him when he ducked under the rope. "That's my girlfriend," he growled and rushed over to them. Angie was sitting on the ground, blood dripping down her face and when he met her gaze, her eyes were blurry.

"Max," she said. "I—"

She burst into tears.

"Where's Brayden?"

She shook her head. "I don't know. I'm sorry. I had him in the seat, and—" Her breath hitched, another sob rising. "I woke up, and my car was gone, and—"

Max's world imploded.

"What do you mean your car was gone?" He knelt in front of her, gripping his thighs and trying to resist the urge to shake her. Where in the fuck was his son?

A paramedic came over, swapping the soaked-through bandage out on her forehead. Angie raised a trembling hand to hold it in place. "He'd buckled in. I checked! And then I closed the door, and—"

Her voice broke.

"Shh," Anna told her. "Everything will be okay," she said. "The police are already looking for Angie's car. It has a tracking chip, and—"

"Everything won't fucking be okay!" Max shouted, part of him hating the way she flinched back, the other gripped by pure terror. "Where is Brayden?" he asked. "Where the fuck is my son?"

"I-I don't know," Angie sobbed. "I—"

"Fuck." He stood, paced away. "*Fuck!*"

"You need to get to the hospital," the paramedic told Angie. "That head wound needs to be looked at."

"No," she said. "Not until we find Brayden."

Max's cell rang, and he scrambled to pick it up without looking at the number. "Hello?"

"Dad?"

Max dropped to his knees. "Where are you? Brayden?"

"I-I'm with Mom," his son said, and the fear in his voice almost killed Max. "She took me to the old house, and—"

"Stay there. Don't go anywhere."

"But she won't wake up."

"Okay, buddy, it will be okay. Just stay on the phone with me." He waved at an officer. "321 Turntree Circle. He was taken there."

The officer nodded, lifting his radio and relaying the address.

"Just keep talking to me, Bray." He said, infinitely calmer now that he could hear Brayden's voice. "Some policemen are going to come to pick you up."

"Why not you?"

"Because they can get there faster, okay? They'll bring you to a police station," he addressed the last as a question to the officer, who nodded. "And I'll meet you there."

"O-okay."

"How long?" he mouthed to the policeman, who indicated five minutes. "Bray, you're going to stay on the phone with me for a few minutes then they'll be there. All right, buddy?"

Brayden's voice was shaky. "Is Angie okay?"

He watched her push to her knees then up to wobbly feet, brushing off Anna's help as she staggered toward him. "Is that—?"

He nodded.

She stumbled to a halt. "Is he okay?"

Max nodded. "Angie's fine, too, bud." He muted his cell, hating that she was wavering on her feet, that blood was once again soaking through the bandage. She wavered on her feet again, and he steadied her. "You need to go—"

"Dad?"

He unmuted the call, waved to Anna, who came over and grabbed Angie's shoulder. "Yeah, bud?"

"There's a police car here."

"Let me talk to them."

He spoke to them briefly, confirming their identities and which station he would meet them at. By the time he hung up, a good five minutes had passed.

Max turned around, wanting to find Angie. To tell her that—

She was gone.

Only Anna was there.

"Where's—?"

Anna shook her head. "Hospital. She wouldn't let me come." She shoved him. "But, and here's some real talk, asshole, I know you were panicked, but she was worried sick and hurting, and you screamed at her then ordered her to leave."

"I—"

"Didn't you tell me that you love her? Didn't you tell her that?" Anna sighed. "You didn't think that maybe couples who love each other try to work things out *together?* You didn't think that maybe she might need some comfort, too?"

"Fuck, Anna. Brayden was gone, and I—"

"Acted like an asshole instead of a rational adult trying to figure out a terrifying situation."

"You know what?" he said as an officer came over and told him they could take his patrol car to the station. "Why don't you go home? Your priority should be Brayden. Not me."

"Yeah," she snapped. "Well, I think you demonstrated *that* fact very clearly to Angie." A pause. "And maybe once you get your head out of your ass, you might find out how badly Angie was injured and make sure *the woman you supposedly love* is okay."

"Fuck off," he growled. He'd seen she was cut on her head and needed stitches.

He'd had more than his share of sutures. They weren't the end of the world.

"No. I think you meant fuck *you*."

And with that, Anna got in her car and drove away.

THIRTY

Angie

ANGIE WOKE up in a hospital room.

Sterile white walls, a line in her arm, and, her eyes drifted around the space . . .

Alone.

Funny. This was becoming a pattern in her life.

If two could be considered a pattern, she supposed.

Regardless, the lights were dim, so Angie guessed it was still nighttime, but the last thing she remembered was being wheeled down the hall for a CT scan. How long had she been out?

Well, apparently her brain was okay because she was alone and only hooked up to one bag of medicine.

Brain damage would require more than that, right?

She reached a hand up then nearly knocked herself unconscious when she found out in a rather painful fashion that her left arm was in a cast.

"Ugh." Using her good arm, she reached for the remote and tilted the bed so she could sit up. The movement made her head pound, but she kept going anyway. Her purse was sitting on the rolling table.

Head spinning, it took incremental movements to bring it closer, but finally she was able to reach her cast-free hand inside and extract her cell.

There were a dozen missed calls from Anna and Mandy, plus text messages and calls from Kelsey. Even the group chain with Cora, Kels, and company was flooded with concerned inquiries.

But the one person she really hoped to hear from had been silent.

She called Mandy first.

Her sister picked up before it even rang once. "Angie? Are you—?"

"I'm okay."

"I'm coming home," Mandy said, and Angie could hear movement in the background. "I knew when I saw Max get off I should have followed, but I got on the damned plane and then I heard and now you're—"

"I'm fine, Mandy. Pinky promise," Angie told her. "Aside from a splitting headache, so if you could take it down a notch that would be great."

"Oh. Sorry."

Angie smiled. "Please, don't apologize. I'm good but tired. Can we talk tomorrow?"

"Of course." She sniffed. "You had me worried there, kid."

"I always pull through."

They exchanged goodbyes and then Angie sent a text to the group chain and Anna, fielding replies and giving assurances for a few minutes.

And then, heart in her throat, she texted Max.

Her response was silence.

Look, she got it. Brayden had been under her supervision. She'd let him down, had put his son at risk, and—

Tears flooded her eyes.

It was *her* fault that Brayden was—

Please, she sent. *Please just tell me if he's okay.*

Finally, what seemed like an eternity later, her cell buzzed with a response.

He's uninjured.

But not okay? She wanted to ask but was too scared. What if he *wasn't* okay? And they'd already established the whole situation was all her fault. If she'd been more aware of her surroundings, if she'd taken up Devon on that ride . . . it might not have happened.

Dammit. She'd been through this before.

She should have known better.

I'm so sorry, Max.

Me too, Angie.

Angie. Not Angel.

As far as painful goodbyes went, that one was at the top of the list.

THIRTY-ONE

Max

"I WANT TO SEE ANGIE," Brayden said, pushing his bowl of cereal away.

It was nine o'clock in the morning and they'd skipped school because being kidnapped by his biological mother seemed like a really good excuse for Bray to play hooky.

"Angie's probably sleeping," Max hedged. "It's still early."

Fuck, but he didn't want to think about Angie or the trickling feeling that Anna was right and he'd acted like an asshole. He needed to do what he should have done in the first place and keep his distance.

Focus on his son.

Suzanne wasn't going to be in the picture again. She'd been unconscious when the police arrived, slumped over the steering wheel, bloodstream full of drugs and alcohol, and damned lucky she hadn't killed Brayden or someone else. Currently, she was detoxing in jail and would be staying in those accommodations for a good long while.

Max might have felt guilty pushing for the harshest punishments for a pregnant woman, but it turned out she wasn't actually pregnant at all. Another ploy, another manipulation.

But this time, it would be accompanied by criminal charges and jail time.

"I want to see Angie!"

"Brayden," he warned.

His son burst into tears. "She's dead, isn't she? Mom killed her, and now I'll never see Angie again, and—"

"What?" Max rounded the table and put his arms around Brayden, holding tight despite the fact that his son tried to push him away. "No. I talked to her last night. She's okay."

Brayden sniffed. "I don't believe you."

"She was hurt, but she texted me last night."

Brayden crossed his arms. "Angie is nice. She likes me and wants to be my friend."

"Bray." Max sighed when his son stuck out his bottom lip.

"She was going to be my new mom, I know it."

Yeah, Max had thought that, too. But that was before he realized that taking his focus off Brayden was a mistake that would put his son at risk.

"She was fun and loves me, and now—" His eyes welled up.

Max said the only thing he could, "Should we check on her?"

Finally, some light appeared in his son's eyes. "Yes! We need to bring her flowers. And a card!" He pushed out of Max's arms. "I'm going to go make her one."

"I meant call . . ." Max trailed off with a sigh.

Sparky padded into the kitchen, eyed the bowl of cereal. Max narrowed his eyes at the dog and took it to the sink before spending a few minutes cleaning up the space. He hadn't slept at all last night, had just sat on the floor next to Bray's bed, listened to his son sleep, and thought about all the ways he could have lost him.

He could have lost Brayden.

He'd had a lucky miss, and now he needed to put all his focus back where it should be.

Max opened the pantry door, put the cereal away, then saw the wrapped box, an envelope adorned with his name taped to it.

"What is—?" That hadn't been there the day before. He knew because Anna had stocked up at the grocery store while Brayden had been at school, and Max had helped her put everything away.

He picked up the box—it rattled and was surprisingly light. He tore open the envelope.

Max,
I know how much you missed these, so I had a work friend pick you up a box when he was in Vancouver. Enjoy your sugar fix, just don't send the team's nutritionist after me.
Love, A

"Fuck."

"That's a bad word."

Max jumped and whirled around. Brayden was fully dressed, card in hand. "I know, bud."

"Oh," Bray said. "Angie asked me where we should hide it." His voice got excited. "She even let me wrap it, and I put it in here because it's food—" He clamped a hand over his mouth. "Sorry," he said, voice muffled. "I almost ruined the surprise."

Max stood there, eviscerated to the core.

He'd thought Angie was a risk? Fuck, but *how* could she be a risk when she was so fucking wonderful with Brayden?

"Dad?" Bray said. "Open it!"

Max tore the paper off, held up the box.

Brayden grinned. "Do you like it?"

"It's only the best cereal *ever*." Something he'd mentioned *once* in passing during their conversations. Something she'd actively gone out of her way to get for him. Something—

"Dammit, Anna was right," he said. "I really fucked up."

"Dad!"

He glanced down at Bray. "Sorry. But I owe Angie a really big apology. I wasn't very nice to her last night."

"You lost your temper?"

Max nodded. "Yeah, but worse. I was so worried about you and scared, that I took it out on her."

Bray's brows pulled down. "That's not cool, Dad."

"No, it wasn't."

And now, shit. How the hell was he going to fix this? How was he going to prove to her that he had room in his life for both her and Brayden? Because it wasn't a space issue . . .

It was a how could he possibly live his life without this incredibly kind, beautiful, and gifted woman issue?

Spoiler alert. The answer was: he couldn't.

"We need to get her really big bouquet of flowers," Brayden said. "And chocolate, and—"

"We'll get all those for sure, bud," Max said as an idea occurred to him, a way that just might show her how important she truly was to him and Brayden. "But we have to make a stop and get a few other things first."

"What things?"

Max told Bray his plan then asked, "What do you think?"

Brayden nodded determinedly. "I think it's perfect."

THIRTY-TWO

Angie

ANGIE HAD JUST COMPLETED A WHOLLY unsatisfying sponge bath—which first, why was it called a freaking bath when she hardly felt any cleaner after it? And second, was wholly *sponge* free—when she met her gaze in her bathroom mirror.

Bruising covered the side of her face but a bandage hid the worst of it—sixteen stitches and two staples in her scalp.

Frankenstein, she was.

Sighing, she dropped her towel then went into her bedroom to slip on a pair of sweats and a hoodie.

This was a no bra and no underwear day, m'kay? She figured she'd earned it.

Especially after the police had come to the hospital last night and taken her statement.

For hours.

Which had been an exercise in uselessness as far as she was concerned, considering that she hadn't seen anything other than a flash of movement.

The only beneficial thing was that she'd found out her attacker had been Suzanne.

No stranger she had to worry about attacking again, no stalker waiting in the bushes, just a deranged ex-wife that would be locked up for a long time.

Which should have been equally concerning, but Angie had already been through this before. She knew she wasn't going to slip back down the path of not living her life, of locking herself away out of fear.

Nope. No way. She'd take some precautions, adjust her bearings, and keep on living.

But how to make Max see that he needed to do the same? Understandably, he had been freaked out last night. His ex-wife had snapped, put his son at risk. That would make anyone panic and lash out.

Not that she was a glutton for punishment or ready to be someone's punching bag. She had worth and deserved to be treated as such, but even the most casual observer had to understand that sometimes there were extenuating circumstances, and Max having his son kidnapped by his crazy ex certainly fit into those.

Angie was ready to put his outburst aside, to move on.

What she wasn't ready for was to give up something precious that she'd fought her fears and anxiety to obtain.

She *finally* had a family, dammit, and she wasn't giving them up.

After struggling with her hoodie zipper for a minute, she managed to get it lined up and zipped.

And not a moment too soon.

Because there was a knock at the door.

She sighed, hurrying over. It was probably Mandy even though she'd told her not to come.

"I'm fine—"

Her words dried up at the sight in front of her.

Two Stormtroopers stood on her threshold.

"Um . . ."

Yes. Not her finest moment of dialogue, but it wasn't often that two cinematic characters stood on her doorstep.

The little one held up a giant bouquet of roses.

Angie took it. "Aren't you a little short for a Stormtrooper?"

She couldn't help it; the situation was just too perfect to not quote a line from the original *Star Wars* film.

(*Star Wars: A New Hope* if she were being technical).

Brayden tore off his helmet, revealing a huge grin. "I knew you'd say that!" He turned and grabbed the other Stormtrooper's hand. "Dad! You were right."

Max started to extend a box in her direction then seemed to notice her hand and halted. He tucked it under his arm then tugged off his helmet. "Hi," he said.

God, he was pretty.

Black hair mussed. Blue eyes bright with emotion.

"Hi."

His lips—the ones she loved to kiss—twitched. "Hi."

They were such dorks, and she loved him so much and so she continued along their usual tack. "Hi."

Brayden pushed by her. "Can we go in now? Where's Sammy? Can I pet him?"

"Sure—" Angie began, but Max cleared his throat and raised a brow. "Bray."

Brayden spun on a dime and launched himself at Angie. "I'm so glad you're okay."

She smiled, hugging him tight, careful to not whack him with her cast or the flowers. "I'm glad *you're* okay. That was scary."

"Yeah." A sage nod.

She bent, whispered, "You need to talk about it?"

"Not yet."

"Okay."

"Can I go see Sammy now?"

"Sure." She pointed to the bedroom. "He was sleeping on the windowsill last I saw."

Brayden tore off down the hall, leaving her alone with Max and suddenly feeling nervous. Maybe this was just a pity visit. Or the precursor to a kiss-off-and-leave-him-alone. Or—

What had that been about her fighting for what she wanted?

Well . . . it had certainly been a lot easier going in her mind.

Max took the flowers from her hands and headed for the kitchen. He found a vase on his second try of her cabinets then plunked the bouquet into the water.

"Here," he said, handing her the box.

"Um."

"Open it first. Then we can—"

His eyes were so serious that she found she had to break the tension. "There better not be confetti in here."

Max shook his head, the barest trace of a smile on his lips. "No confetti."

She tore one corner of the wrapping paper, stopped, and sighed. "Why am I so nervous?"

He took her good hand, used it to continue tearing the paper off. "Because I was a total jackass, and you deserved better. I was panicked, but—"

"I get it—" she began.

"Well, I don't." He tossed the paper aside. "You're important, Angel. And fuck, but I love you so much. Last night was . . . a supremely shitty way to show it. I was out of my mind and horrible and—"

"Max."

"I need you to see," he said, "that I will never treat you like that again. I was all ramped up and ready to play the martyr, to try and survive without you because it would be quote-unquote better for me to focus on my son."

Her heart twisted. Maybe that was better?

"I—"

"But you know what I realized? This morning, I saw your gift. Just cereal, but so you—thoughtful and sweet." He shook his head. "It wasn't just the gift itself. Brayden was so excited because you included him in it. Same as he was thrilled to go with you to the game last night and to invite you to the concert." His hands were trembling now, the box rattling in their shared hold. "I realized that you don't just make my life better. You make Brayden's life better, too."

She inhaled rapidly. "I love you both. But I understand if you need to keep it just the two of you. I'd like to be friends with you and him at the very least, but—"

"Open it." He inclined his chin toward the box, which was now paper-free, but the plain cardboard did nothing to reveal its contents.

Angie gave him a questioning look.

What was in that damned box that was so important?

His eyes warmed. "Never mind. I'll do it." And he took off the lid.

"*Oh.*" She sniffed, tears immediately welling up. "Dammit!" She smacked him, but it wasn't out of anger. She was so incredibly touched, and now he was going to turn her into a watering pot.

Because inside that box was the cartoon drawing from an artist on the pier. The one who drew little caricatures of people and families. Only this one had been done in the theme of *Star Wars*.

Max was there, along with Brayden, Anna, and Sparky.

And Angie was there, too.

She was in their family drawing.

"Fuck," she sniffed, wiping her eyes.

Because Sammy was there, too.

"Fuck's a bad word," Brayden said, coming up behind her and surprising her with another hug. "Don't worry, you're not in trouble. Dad says it more."

She met Max's amused gaze. "It's true," he said with a shrug.

Brayden tugged her good hand. "Do you like it?"

"I love it so much," she told him.

"And you'll be part of our family?"

"I would love that more than anything in the world."

He smiled and Max set the box down on her kitchen counter. "Go play with Sammy for a few minutes. I'm going to kiss Angie now."

"Ew."

Brayden ran back down the hall.

"Really?" she asked, raising a brow. "You had to tell him that?"

"He'll need to get used to the idea," Max said, tugging her close. "I plan on kissing you a lot."

Her lips curved. "Yeah?"

He nuzzled the curve of her jaw, nibbled at her ear lobe. "Yeah."

"Cool," she said, affecting Brayden's tone.

They both burst into laughter, Max's hot breath on her neck making her shiver. "I thought you were going to kiss me," she teased when they both had regained control of themselves.

"That's the plan," he told her and cupped her face in both palms. "I just—I don't want you to forgive me so easily. I was a real ass—"

She cupped one of his cheeks in turn, the unwieldy cast getting in her way on the other. "Damn, you really are determined to hold on to that martyr card, huh?" Her lips found his for a short kiss. "I was already cooking up a plan because I wasn't going to let you push me away from the best thing in my life."

"*Thing?*" he asked. "You mean Brayden?"

"No," she said then hurried to add before he could misinterpret her, "I mean, he's wonderful, but what I *really* meant was that I wasn't going to let you push me away from my family." She smiled. "Luckily for us both, you came to your senses before I had to jump you and force you to see reason."

Max paused, head tilting as though considering. "How exactly were you going to jump me?"

Angie snorted. "Don't you want to know?"

"I do," he said, laughing. "I really do."

"Maybe I'll show you sometime," she teased, bringing her mouth close and her body flush to his. Her breasts brushed his chest, her pelvis pressed firmly against the hard ridge of his erection.

"Torturing me?" He raised a brow when she grinned.

"You like it."

"I do."

"So"—she tapped a finger to her chin—"when's that kissing coming?"

He opened his mouth, ready with another quip, then closed it and shook his head. Because puns and teasing and jokes didn't matter. Not when his woman wanted him to kiss her. And so he brought his lips to hers and kissed her—soft, sweet, almost leisurely.

"Now," he told her, when he paused to let her breathe. "And forever."

She wrapped her good arm around his neck, rose up on tiptoe.

"That I can live with."

And then he kissed her again.

EPILOGUE

Blue, Six Months Later

BLUE WALKED into Max's backyard, his latest girl on his arm.

He'd met her at the bar last night and they'd fucked like rabbits until the sun came up. Then they'd fucked some more.

Now, he was making the requisite appearance at Max's engagement party.

He was happy for his friends . . . for all of them.

But fuck, he was the last of the guys.

The final holdout.

The only single one.

Which wasn't really a fair assessment because there were other guys on the team who were single or divorced, but Blue wasn't that close to them.

Not like he was with Brit, Stefan, Blane, and Max.

They had been his people from his rookie season, and they'd taken him under their respective wings.

And now they were all married or engaged or had cute little babies.

Yes, he got that he was younger than them, knew that he had plenty of time to sow his wild oats and still have a family.

But all Blue knew was that it was getting damned old coming home to an empty house all the time.

"There are kids here," his date Bindi—or Bambi or Bobbi, because fuck if he could remember—said and her tone told him that she equated children with the seventh circle of hell.

"Yeah," he said. "The guys have a lot of kids."

Her face puckered with disgust, and suddenly Blue wasn't remembering how good of a hand job Bindi or Bambi or Bobbi could give, but how happy Angie had been when Max had proposed on the Golden Gate Bridge.

Blue wanted *that*.

Not *this*.

"You know what?" he said, taking Bindi or Bambi or Bobbi's hand in his and tugging her toward the front of the house, while he pulled out his cell with his other. "This will be lame. Why don't I text you later when I'm done?"

Calling an Uber took seconds.

Untangling the octopus Bindi or Bambi or Bobbi upon the car's arrival took longer.

Much longer.

But finally, he managed to pack her into the car and sighed with relief as it drove away.

Until he turned and saw *her*.

Anna.

Who always looked at him with glarey eyes and a pissy expression.

"There's my Ice Queen," he said, moving past her and heading back to the party. He'd congratulate the couple then go the fuck back to his empty apartment.

"Doesn't it get old?" Anna asked, trailing after him.

"Doesn't *what* get old?" he countered, snagging a beer from a nearby table.

"Being a fucking sleaze."

Blue froze then shook his head. "You don't know me."

Anna rolled her eyes. "I know *plenty* of guys like you. Fuck anything that moves, never sleep with the same girl twice, and too wrapped up in your own damned cock to be a good lay."

She'd gotten his rage pretty ramped until the last statement.

That last one though?

It had tempered his anger.

He was good in bed. *Really* fucking good. In fact, Blue made it a point to make sure anyone he slept with had a better time than him. And that wasn't ego talking, sex just wasn't fun for him if his partner didn't orgasm at least twice.

He was an overachiever, what could he say?

Ah. Now *there* was his ego talking.

Smirking, Blue tapped his chin. "Sounds like a personal problem to me. Maybe you're too cold in the sack to enjoy yourself. Or maybe you freeze a guys' cock off with your Ice Princess powers."

Anna huffed. "You're unbelievable, you know that?"

Blue jerked his chin toward the front of the house. "That's what *she* said."

As Anna flounced off, Blue couldn't stop himself from watching her ass, because as much as he teased her about being icy during their interactions, he had the feeling she was very much fire under all that frost.

Not that he'd find out.

He and Anna were oil and water, two tomcats fighting over territory or, metaphors aside, they just always managed to get on each other's nerves.

And while he couldn't deny she was hot and gorgeous, Blue

wanted a little more peace in his life when he found the right woman.

He wanted a girlfriend who didn't constantly poke and antagonize but was sweet and gentle and kind. Like Sara. Like Angie. Yes, that made him an egotistical asshole—that he wanted a pretty and nice girl at home—but there it was.

Blue had enough stress in his career that he wanted to keep it simple at home.

Who could fault him for that?

He socialized for a while, congratulating the happy couple and wishing them the best, played with Max's son, Brayden, on the trampoline for a bit—which turned out to be a lot longer than a bit because once one kid saw him use the platform to launch Brayden in the air, Blue suddenly was begged and pleaded by all the kiddos to have a turn.

And then another.

So, by the time he dragged his tired ass out of the trampoline, the party was breaking up.

He said his goodbyes and headed for the driveway, pulling out his cell for Uber round two.

"Baby Blues." He turned, saw Anna getting into a Prius. "Need a ride?"

He raised his brows. "You going to freeze my balls off?"

A sexy smile. "You know it."

"I think I'll take my chances with the Uber."

"Chicken."

Blue rolled his eyes. "Seriously?"

"Buck-buck," she clucked. "Buck-buck-*buuuck*."

"You're unbelievable."

"You're a chicken." She sat down in the driver's seat, started to close the door.

Blue sighed, sought patience from heaven. It didn't matter what she said.

But then his eyes drifted back over to her car, and she was looking at him with that annoying ass smirk. "Fine," he grumbled and stomped over to her Prius, opening the door and dropping down into the passenger's seat with a huff.

"Was that so terrible?" she teased.

"The worst."

Anna flicked on the radio, filling the airwaves with classic rock. Which surprised him—he'd figured she would be more of a pop girl. But before he could ask her about it, she turned up the volume and backed out of the driveway.

He had to shout directions to his place over the noise, but that was probably her intention. And it wasn't like he lived far or that they were complicated.

Hell, he should probably be grateful that she'd saved him the extra aggravation of having to converse with her.

Ten minutes later, she pulled into his driveway and put the car into park.

Only then did she turn down the volume.

"Your humble abode," she said, sweeping a hand toward the little cottage tucked into a hillside south of San Francisco. It was ridiculously expensive and still mostly empty, but it was home and, as an army brat, probably the most settled he'd ever been in his whole life.

"Yup," he said, reaching for the handle. "Thanks for the ride."

"Try not to go out and get a fresh bimbo to ride tonight. I hear STIs on are the rise in the city."

Blue sighed, turned back to face her. "Really?"

She shrugged, smirk teasing the edges of her mouth, drawing his focus to the lushness of her lips. "Just watching out for Max's teammate."

He rolled his eyes. "Not hardly."

"Okay, how about I'm trying to prevent you from spreading STIs to the female populace."

"I'm clean, and I'm smart," he told her. "Condoms all the way."

"Ew."

Except there was something about the way she said it that made Blue stiffen and take notice. Because . . . he stared into her eyes, watched as the pale blue darkened to royal, saw her lips part, and her suck in a breath.

Holy shit.

"You're attracted to me."

Her jaw dropped. "No fucking way," she said, too quickly, pink dancing on the edges of her cheekbones. "You're delusional."

Blue got close.

Real close.

Anna licked her lips.

And fuck it all, he kissed that luscious mouth.

—*Breakaway, Gold Hockey Book 5 is now available!*

GOLD HOCKEY SERIES

Blocked

Backhand

Boarding

Benched

Breakaway

Breakout

Checked

GOLD HOCKEY

Did you miss any of the Gold Hockey books?
Find information about the full series here.
Or keep reading for a sneak peek into each of the books below!

Blocked
Gold Hockey Book #1
Get your copy at books2read.com/Blocked

Brit

THE FIRST QUESTION Brit always got when people found out she played ice hockey was *"Do you have all of your teeth?"*

The second was *"Do you, you know, look at the guys in the locker room?"*

The first she could deal with easily—flash a smile of her full set of chompers, no gaps in sight. The second was more problematic. Especially since it was typically accompanied by a smug smile or a coy wink.

Of course she looked. *Everybody* looked once. Everyone

snuck a glance, made a judgment that was quickly filed away and shoved deep down into the recesses of their mind.

And she meant *way* down.

Because, dammit, she was there to play hockey, not assess her teammates' six packs. If she wanted to get her man candy fix, she could just go on social media. There were shirtless guys for days filling her feed.

But that wasn't the answer the media wanted.

Who cared about locker room dynamics? Who gave a damn whether or not she, as a typical heterosexual woman, found her fellow players attractive?

Yet for some inane reason, it *did* matter to people.

Brit wasn't stupid. The press wanted a story. A scandal. They were desperate for her to fall for one of her teammates—or better yet the captain from their rival team—and have an affair that was worthy of a romantic comedy.

She'd just gotten very good at keeping her love life—as nonexistent as it was—to herself, gotten very good at not reacting in any perceptible way to the insinuations.

So when the reporter asked her the same set of questions for the thousandth time in her twenty-six years, she grinned—showing off those teeth—and commented with a sweetly innocent "Could've sworn you were going to ask me about the coed showers." She waited for the room-at-large to laugh then said, "Next question, please."

–Get your copy at books2read.com/Blocked

Backhand
Gold Hockey Book #2
Get your copy at books2read.com/Backhand

Sara

"Sorry I messed up your sketch," he rumbled.

She nibbled on the side of her mouth, biting back a smile. "Sorry I stole your hand for so long."

He shrugged. "My mom's an artist. I get it."

Well, there went her battle with the smile. Her lips twitched and her teeth came out of hiding. If there was one thing that Sara had, it was her smile. It had been her trademark in her competition days.

Which were long over.

Her mouth flattened out, the grin slipping away. Time to go, time to forget, to move on, to rebuild. "Thanks," she said and extended a hand.

Then winced and dropped it when her ribs cried out in protest.

"You okay?" he asked, head tilting, eyes studying her.

"Fine." And out popped her new smile. The fake one. Careful of her aching side, she shrugged into her backpack. "I've got to go." She turned, ponytail flapping through the hair to land on her opposite shoulder.

"That—" He touched her arm. "Wait. I *know* I know you."

She froze. That was the second time he'd said that, and now they were getting into dangerous territory. Recognition meant . . . no. She couldn't.

There had been a time when *everyone* had known her. Her face on Wheaties boxes, her smile promoting toothpaste and credit cards alike.

That wasn't her life any longer.

"Thanks again. Bye." She started to hurry away.

"Wait." A hand dropped on to her shoulder, thwarting her escape, and she hissed in pain.

"Sorry," he said, but he didn't release her. Instead, he shifted his grip from her aching shoulder down to her elbow and when she didn't protest, he exerted gentle pressure until Sara was facing him again. "It's just that know I *know* you."

No. This wasn't happening.

"You're Sara Jetty."

Her body went tense.

Oh God. This was *so* happening.

"It's me." He touched his chest like she didn't know he was talking about himself, and even as she was finally recognizing the color of his eyes, the familiar curve of his lips and line of his jaw, he said the worst thing ever, "Mike Stewart."

Oh *shit.*

—Get your copy at books2read.com/Backhand

Boarding
Gold Hockey Book #3
Get your copy at books2read.com/Boarding

HOCKEY PLAYERS HAD the *best* asses.

No pancake bottoms, these men—and *women*—could fill out a pair of jeans. She wanted to squeeze it, to nibble it, bounce a dime—

Mandy dropped her chin to her chest, losing sight of the Sorting Hat cupcakes she'd been pondering.

Blane with his yummy ass had a unique way of distracting her.

No, it wasn't even distraction, per se. He had *always* been able to get under her skin.

And that was very, very bad for her.

"Ugh," she said, tossing her phone onto her desk and standing, knowing that she wouldn't be able to sit still now.

Nope, she needed about forty laps in the pool and a good hard fu—

Run, her mind blurted, almost yelling at the mental voice of her inner devil. *A good hard run.*

Unfortunately, the cajoling tone wasn't completely drowned out. *Some sexy horizontal time with Blane would be more fun—*

But the rest of the enticing words were lost as the roar of the crowd suddenly penetrated through the layers of concrete. Her stomach twisted. Mandy could tell, even before her eyes made it to the television, that it wasn't in celebration of a goal or a good hit either.

This was fury, a collective of outrage.

She was on her feet the moment she saw the prone form lying so still face down on the ice.

Her gut twisted when she spotted the curving line of a numeral two on the back of the player's jersey.

"Not him," she said and the words were familiar, a sentiment she had whispered, had *prayed* a thousand times before. She needed the camera angle to shift, for her to be able to see more clearly *who* was hurt. "Not him."

Then Dr. Carter was on the ice and the player moved slightly, rolling away from the camera, giving a full shot of his back and the matching twos adorning his jersey.

Fuck. Not him. Not Blane.

And that was when she saw the pool of blood.

—Get your copy at books2read.com/Boarding

Benched
Gold Hockey Book #4

Get your copy at books2read.com/Benched

Max

He started up the car, listening and chiming in at the right places as Brayden talked all things video game.

But his mind was unfortunately stuck on the fact that women were not to be trusted.

He snorted. Brit—the Gold's goalie and the first female in the NHL—and Mandy—the team's head trainer—would smack him around for that sentiment, so he silently amended it to: *most* women were not to be trusted.

There. Better, see?

Somehow, he didn't think they'd see.

He parked in the school's lot, walked Brayden in, and received the appropriate amount of scorn from the secretary for being thirty minutes late to school, then bent to hug Brayden.

"I'll pick you up today," he said.

Brayden smiled and hugged him tightly. Then he whispered something in his ear that hit Max harder than a two-by-four to the temple.

"If you got me a new mom, we wouldn't be late for school."

"Wh-what?" Max stammered.

"Please, Dad? Can you?"

And with that mind fuck of an ask, Brayden gave him one more squeeze and pushed through the door to the playground, calling, "Love you!" over his shoulder.

Then he was gone, and Max was standing in the office of his son's school struggling to comprehend if he had actually just heard what he'd heard.

A new mom?

Fuck his life.

—Get your copy at books2read.com/Benched

Breakaway
Gold Hockey Book #5
Get your copy at books2read.com/BreakawayGold

Blue

"Thanks for the ride."

"Try not to go out and get a fresh bimbo to ride tonight. I hear STIs on are the rise in the city."

Blue sighed, turned back to face her. "Really?"

She shrugged, smirk teasing the edges of her mouth, drawing his focus to the lushness of her lips. "Just watching out for Max's teammate."

He rolled his eyes. "Not hardly."

"Okay, how about I'm trying to prevent you from spreading STIs to the female populace."

"I'm clean, and I'm smart," he told her. "Condoms all the way."

"Ew."

Except there was something about the way she said it that made Blue stiffen and take notice. Because . . . he stared into her eyes, watched as the pale blue darkened to royal, saw her lips part, and her suck in a breath.

Holy shit.

"You're attracted to me."

Her jaw dropped. "No fucking way," she said, too quickly, pink dancing on the edges of her cheekbones. "You're delusional."

Blue got close.

Real close.

Anna licked her lips.

And fuck it all, he kissed that luscious mouth.

—Breakaway, www.books2read.com/BreakawayGold

Breakout

Gold Hockey Book #6
Get your copy at books2read.com/Breakout

PR-Rebecca

A fucking perfect hockey fairy tale.

Shaking her head, because she knew firsthand that fairy tales didn't exist outside of rom-coms and occasionally between alpha sports heroes and their chosen mates, Rebecca slipped through the corridor and stepped onto the Gold's bench.

Lots of dudes in suits—of both the boardroom *and* the hockey variety—were hugging.

On the ice. Near the goals. On the bench.

It was a proverbial hug-fest.

And she was the cynical bitch who couldn't enjoy the fact that the team she was with had just won the biggest hockey prize of them all.

"I knew you'd be like this."

Rebecca turned her focus from Brit, who was skating with the huge silver cup, to the man—no, to the *boy* because no matter how pretty and yummy he was, Kevin was still a decade younger than her—leaning oh so casually against the boards.

"Nice goal," she told him.

A shrug. "Blue made a nice pass."

And dammit, the fact that he wasn't an arrogant son of a bitch made her like him more.

She nodded at the cup. "You should go have your turn."

"I'll get mine," he said with another shrug.

She frowned, honestly confused. "You don't want—"

Suddenly he was in front of her on the bench, towering over her even though she was wearing her four-inch power heels. "You know what I want?"

Rebecca couldn't speak. Her breath had whooshed out of her in the presence of all that sweaty, hockey god-ness. Fuck he was pretty and gorgeous and . . . so fucking masculine that her thighs actually clenched together.

She wanted to climb him like a stripper pole.

"Do you?" he asked again when her words wouldn't come. "Want to know what I want?"

She nodded.

He bent, lips to her ear. "You, babe," he whispered. "I. Want. You."

Then he straightened and jumped back onto the ice, leaving her gaping after him like she had less than two brain cells in her skull.

The worst part?

She wanted him, too.

Had wanted him since the moment she'd laid eyes on the sexy as sin hockey god.

"Trouble," she murmured. "I'm in *so* much fucking trouble."

—Breakout, www.books2read.com/breakout

Checked
Gold Hockey Book #7
Get your copy at books2read.com/Checked

"Rebecca."

She kept walking.

She might work with Gabe, but she sure as heck wasn't on speaking terms with him. He'd dismissed her work, ignored her contribution to the team. He'd made her feel small and unimportant and—

She kept walking.

"*Rebecca.*"

Not happening. Her car was in sight, thank fuck. She beeped the locks, reached for the handle.

He caught her arm.

"Baby—"

"I am *not* your baby, and you don't get to touch me." She ripped herself free, started muttering as she reached for the handle of her car again. "You don't even like me."

He stepped close, real close. Not touching her, not pushing the boundary she'd set, and yet he still got really freaking close. Her breath caught, her chin lifted, her pulse picked up. "That. Is. Where. You're. Wrong."

She froze.

"What?"

His mouth dropped to her ear, still not touching, but near enough that she could feel his hot breath.

"I like you, Rebecca. Too fucking much."

Then he turned and strode away.

—Checked, coming March 29th, 2020, www.books2read.com/Checked

Breakout

Checked (March 29th, 2020)

Chauvinist Stories

Bitch (Feb 16th, 2020)

Cougar (March 1st, 2020)

Whore (March 15th, 2020)

Life Sucks Series (all stand alone)

Train Wreck

Phoenix Series

Phoenix Rising

Dark Phoenix

Phoenix Freed

Phoenix: LexTal Chronicles (rereleasing soon, stand alone, Phoenix world)

From Ashes

KTS Series

Fire and Ice (Hurt Anthology, stand alone)

ABOUT THE AUTHOR

USA Today bestselling author, Elise Faber, loves chocolate, Star Wars, Harry Potter, and hockey (the order depending on the day and how well her team -- the Sharks! -- are playing). She and her husband also play as much hockey as they can squeeze into their schedules, so much so that their typical date night is spent on the ice. Elise is the mom to two exuberant boys and lives in Northern California. Connect with her in her Facebook group, the Fabinators or find more information about her books at www.elisefaber.com.

f facebook.com/elisefaberauthor

a amazon.com/author/elisefaber

BB bookbub.com/profile/elise-faber

instagram.com/elisefaber

g goodreads.com/elisefaber

pinterest.com/elisefaberwrite

Made in the USA
Monee, IL
26 October 2021